SHE WAS JUST SEVENTEEN

SHE WAS JUST SEVENTEEN

by

Bob Black

Dales Large Print Books
Long Preston, North Yorkshire,
BD23 4ND, England.

British Library Cataloguing in Publication Data.

Black, Bob
    She was just seventeen.

    A catalogue record of this book is
    available from the British Library

    ISBN   1-84262-362-1 pbk

First published in Great Britain in 2003 by D.C. Thomson

Published in Large Print 2005 by arrangement with
Mr Robert Black

Dales Large Print is an imprint of Library Magna Books Ltd.

Printed and bound in Great Britain by
T.J. (International) Ltd., Cornwall, PL28 8RW

CHAPTER ONE

John-Joseph Delaney hated flying. He always had. Few things in the world could entice him on to a plane.

Yet here he was, having spent 19 of the last 24 hours in the air, travelling from Sydney, Australia; to Singapore; and then on to London.

He'd hated every minute of it.

At least his nightmare was almost over. This was the final leg of what had been an interminable journey.

'Would passengers please fasten their seat-belts and ensure that their seats are returned to the upright position. Thank you!'

He didn't need telling twice. He was already sitting rigidly upright and had been for most of the flight; a sandy-haired, middle-aged man, unduly tight-lipped and reserved and belted, with breathtaking ferocity, into his seat.

His hands gripped the armrests tightly, and there was a familiar, nervous fluttering in his stomach.

The plane banked steeply into its final descent.

Far below, the twinkling lights of Liverpool were scattered across the dark earth like a constellation of electric stars.

Below, too, was the reason he had felt compelled to travel halfway round the world. Somewhere down there was the answer to a question that had haunted him for 40 years.

This high up in the air John-Joseph was easily fooled into believing that this would be a Liverpool he knew and recognised.

The belief sustained him for all of an hour.

It took his mind off the anxious landing in the dark – the thump of the wheels on the runway. and the headlong rush of the aircraft through the night for what seemed eternity.

His more fearful thoughts were replaced with a warm glow of nostalgia, with memories of childhood and the spirited days of his youth. With a reassuring sense of coming home...

Sydney, Australia, was where he lived now, but even after all this time he still thought of Liverpool as home.

Once on the ground, and in the taxi from the airport to his hotel, he quickly realised that he had been fooling himself. Not only was Liverpool a city full of strangers – the city was a stranger to him.

He didn't recognise the place at all!

But what had he expected? He hadn't set foot in the port since he was 18. Forty years ago.

Even so, the thought that few of the people and places he remembered so fondly were here any more, suddenly struck him with an almost physical force. The terrible realisation, that the charmed city of his youth no longer existed, chilled him to the bone.

For the first time, he considered the

possibility that his mission here was doomed to failure.

Liverpool, his Liverpool, was gone...

His Liverpool. 1962. A city that drank Coke; ate Football; breathed Music. A city with its own special smell in the air, a mixture of the sea and American cigarettes.

It was a city of optimism; of young girls in colourful clothes with wide, bright plastic belts. Above-the-knee shift dresses. Beehives and bobs. Boys in leather jackets, Chelsea boots, and smart three-buttoned suits.

It was a city with a singular awareness of itself, where hair got longer as skirts got shorter; where kids revelled in the thrill of being young and alive; as if no-one had ever been young and alive in the history of the world before.

And they hadn't been. Not like this. Because this was Liverpool.

A city with its own unique heartbeat – The Mersey Beat.

In illicit bars and late-night coffee clubs.

In ballrooms and civic halls. It burgeoned in the bohemian Art College and the dingy basements of Dockland warehouses.

The Beat. It flooded the daytime streets and night-time alleys, where jive clubs and jazz cellars were quickly re-invented and immersed themselves in this new phenomenon.

The phenomenon of The Mersey Beat.

Everywhere there seemed to be the twang of guitars and the click of Cuban heels on cobblestones. Round every corner some new band was practising. Jukeboxes and radios played the latest Eps, LPs, 45s; plastic currency that bought the youth of the day a sense of freedom and a sense of belonging.

To everyone who knew him he was JonJo. To his family and friends. To the local police, who knew him rather well, and the local priest who hardly knew him at all.

It was 'JonJo'. Always 'JonJo'. A wild card. A scally. Not in any unkind, heartless way. In an 18-year-old Liverpool way. Everyone who was anyone was a character. A comic or a poet; a philosopher or a clown; touched with greatness – or just touched.

JonJo had been all of those, and more. And he'd been in love – with Abby.

She was just 17, a straight-'A' student with hidden depths of daring beneath her sweet, shy smile. The kind of girl-next-door he'd never lived next door to.

Under her cotton blouse or sweater dress she was full of fire, full of fun, full of surprises. 'Nice girls' didn't dance the way she did. But they must have done, because she was nice.

She was quiet, she was crazy, she was cool.
And she was JonJo's. Just like Liverpool.
Liverpool, in 1962. His city.
His, and The Beatles.

And look at it now, John-Joseph thought, gazing out the window of his expensive hotel suite. We're like old friends who don't recognise each other.

At that moment he wondered if he really had gone mad. People in Australia seemed to think so. Miss Rodwell certain did. She'd said as much, six weeks ago.

'There's no fool like an old fool!' his secretary of 17 years had reprimanded him.

'Correction! There's no fool like an old fool in love!' she'd gone on.

'Correction! There's no fool like an old fool who was once in love and who is unable – or unwilling – to move on, to break with the past, and give himself the chance to live again, love again, in the present!'

'Are you done, Roddy?' He'd sighed. 'Or have you any more clichés you'd like to hit me with before I leave?'

No. No more clichés, she'd thought to herself. Except the biggest one of all – the one about the spinster secretary who is secretly, devotedly, in love with her employer.

But she'd said none of that. Instead, she'd asked, in disbelief. 'Are you really going to go through with this? Early retirement? Giving up everything you've worked so hard for?'

'Too hard, Roddy, and for too long!'

He'd stood at the window of the room, the conference room of the successful trading company he'd built from nothing, and gazed out across the bay towards the, now very familiar, Opera House and Sydney Harbour Bridge.

'My heart's not in it any more. And I think I've finally realised why. Because I left my heart somewhere in England a long time ago.'

She'd sighed in return, exasperated by the thought of intelligent men who, approaching 60, suddenly and gracelessly, launched themselves willy-nilly into a second adolescence.

'And you're going back to look for it, are you?' she'd said, but not completely without sympathy. 'You're going to fly to England – fly, mind you, and you know how you feel about planes – to look for this girl you were in love with almost forty years ago?'

'I thought I might. There's something I need to ask her.'

'And nothing I can say will make you change your mind?'

'You know very well, Roddy,' he'd said, 'that in the thirty-odd years it's taken me to build this company, there's no-one's advice I've taken more than yours. You mean more to me than anyone here. More to me than either of the women I almost married.

'But this is something I have to do. Can't you try to understand?'

She did understand. Of course she did. Because she would have done anything, gone anywhere, flown to the moon, for John-Joseph Delaney.

By comparison, a trip to Liverpool, England, didn't seem so unreasonable.

'I'll make the arrangements.'

'Thank you.'

'I just hope she's worth all this.'

'She is, Roddy. All this – and more.'

They were together, in all, for a year. Only a year. Each day, when school finished, she waited for him outside the College of Art and they walked home together.

'What's it like? In there?' she asked.

JonJo shrugged. He'd never given it much thought.

15

'It's OK, I suppose,' he said. 'I'm stuck in "still life" at the moment. It's a bit of a yawn, really.

'I wanna design posters, an' magazine covers, an' murals like in the Jacaranda Coffee Bar! Excitin' stuff, y'know?'

'Even so,' Abby said. "Still life" has got to be more excitin' than shorthand an' typin! I mean they're always the same! Dead borin'!'

'Tell you what, then.' JonJo grinned. 'When I'm a famous designer, or "muralist" ... you can be my secretary. You'll run my studio an' my gallery, an' you'll fall in love with me an' never let on.'

Suddenly Abby let go of his hand and stopped in her tracks. She looked serious. Too serious.

'I'm sorry, JonJo,' she said gravely. 'That's not gonna happen. It can't.'

'Why not?' He was almost afraid to ask. His heart sank, as if it went all the way down to his boots on a piece of elastic.

Abby looked anxious.

''Cos I've already fallen in love with you.

That's why!'

The elastic shot JonJo's heart back up into his throat. He could hardly speak.

'Have you?'

She nodded.

'Well … when did that happen?' he asked.

'I don't know really. I wasn't payin' attention.'

'Well, you should've been,' he admonished her. 'These things are important. To tell our grandkids!'

It was Abby's turn to be taken aback.

'Grandkids!? An' I thought I was rushin' things.'

JonJo shrugged. 'All I know is that I never want this to end.'

And they kissed there in the street, with Liverpool and the endless possibilities of their young lives wrapped around them.

With the unique myopia enjoyed by teenagers in love, all JonJo cared about was being with her. All he thought about was the next time they could be together. And then the next.

And he realised, with a jolt, that what he couldn't think about was losing her. And what he couldn't contemplate was a future without her.

Of course, in the end, he hadn't merely contemplated a future without Abby. He'd lived it.

Their lives had taken a dramatically different direction from the one he'd expected.

And now, exhausted; sleepless; tormented by intolerable jet-lag, John-Joseph set about changing direction again.

He'd never seen a private detective before.

Correction! Private investigator, as they apparently preferred to be called.

Either way, his experience of them was strictly limited to TV shows and films.

When he met Harry Carp next morning over breakfast, John-Joseph's first impression was that the man was certainly no Humphrey Bogart. To be honest, he looked more like Peter Lorre.

But behind those heavily-lidded eyes there

was a fierce intelligence and a sincere, apologetic manner.

'I'm sorry, Mr Delaney,' he said quietly. 'When we first spoke on the phone six weeks ago, I was hopeful. But I'm afraid I've had no luck.'

'No luck? You haven't found any trace of her at all?'

'None. And, believe me, I've tried everything. Medical records. Police. DVLA. Registry offices. Passport centre.

'She isn't on the voters' list. But then, if she's married, she'll have changed her name.

'I've checked the records of marriages, divorces, and deaths.'

'She can't just have disappeared!'

'Not deliberately, no,' the investigator said. 'But people move around a lot these days. They marry Perhaps more than once. They separate. Emigrate.

'They ... die,' he said tactfully.

John-Joseph shook his head quickly. 'No. No, she's not dead.'

'And she hasn't really disappeared either,'

Carp said. 'She could be living quite happily on the other side of the world, or just round the corner. I could find her tomorrow, or never.'

'Some people just slip through the net. And it has been a very long time.'

'Forty years.' John-Joseph sighed. 'The blink of an eye.'

He pushed his breakfast plate away, his appetite completely ruined.

'Keep looking,' he said. 'However long it takes. Whatever it costs.'

Harry Carp nodded and got to his feet.

'And if I should find her,' he said. 'Are you sure she'll want to see you, after all this time?'

John-Joseph couldn't answer. He wasn't sure. But that wouldn't stop him looking.

They shook hands across the table. Carp hesitated, as if wanting to make up somehow for all the cold water he'd poured on the man's dream.

'She must be someone … very special,' he said.

'She is,' John-Joseph agreed. 'And was,

from the very first moment I saw her.'

The first time he saw her she was standing outside The Cavern in the rain, a cardigan over her slender shoulders, a glow of anticipation on her pretty face.

She was there with an older cousin.

He was there with his mates; his crowd – the Bold Street Boys.

Bomber. Sunny, funny, six foot three, and built like a piece of string. Still wore drainpipes. And looked like a drainpipe! His genuine American baseball boots made his feet look enormous!

Dillon. Mad as a monkey. He'd do anything for a dare except drag himself out of bed in the mornings. Smoked like a chimney. So he kind of smelled like one, too.

And Colin. Never the sharpest tool in the box, but the kindest. Had a heart of gold. And a conscience big enough for all four of them.

JonJo had christened them the Bold Street Boys. It was in Bold Street they'd first seen

21

a band of four raw fellows, exactly like themselves, with guitars and a drum kit. Except they weren't like themselves at all. They weren't like anybody else.

They were The Beatles, and they were about to change the world.

Now crowds would gather, hundreds deep, to pack The Cavern, a dark subterranean back-street club, when the 'fab four' appeared.

Jostled, Jon-Jo bumped into the girl beside him. He turned to apologise and tumbled headlong into a pair of hazlenut eyes. How could they be so dark and yet so dazzling?

Abby Clark laughed at this good-looking boy, struck dumb before her, then she was swept away as The Cavern doors opened and the crowd surged in.

JonJo looked for her all night but didn't see her again.

Two weeks later, in NEMS, a city centre record shop, she materialised again.

JonJo was at the counter, clutching The Beatles first single, Love Me Do, with its paper sleeve and bright red label. Abby had come in to buy the same record.

'Sorry, luv,' the girl behind the counter said. 'You're outta luck. This fella's taken the last copy. We'll have it in again next week – on Monday.'

Abby turned to go, and as she did she smiled at JonJo. 'Hope you enjoy it,' she said, and she really meant it.

She was smashing.

And JonJo wanted to do the right thing. He desperately wanted to be noble. He wanted to give her the record, make the gesture, the ultimate teenage sacrifice.

But The Beatles were The Beatles.

And he just couldn't do it.

Then inspiration struck. He ran from the shop and caught up with her outside.

'You could come round my place to hear it if you want,' he blurted out. 'Any time. Today. Tomorrow. Saturday!'

'Ta very much,' she said. 'I'd like that.'

JonJo had been holding his breath till she spoke.

23

'Fab!' he gasped, overwhelmed. 'See you there then!'

And he turned to go.

'Don't you think you'd better tell me where you live then?' Abby called after him, laughing that joyful laugh of hers.

JonJo wanted the ground to open up and swallow him. But he was glad it didn't. Because, looking at her, he realised he'd never seen anyone as beautiful as she was. Right there. Right then.

At the beginning of it all.

This, on the other hand, was where it ended. The taxi dropped John-Joseph in front of the house. The house where Abby had lived with her parents in comfortable middle-class suburbia, on the other side of the river from JonJo's home.

It was at this little garden gate – or one exactly like it – she'd said goodbye. It was here she'd told him it was over. Here she'd said the cruellest things, insisting she never wanted to see him again. Here she'd made it clear she didn't love him any more.

He'd argued; pleaded – and cried.

He'd tried to follow her inside, and when the door was shut in his face he'd hammered on it for almost an hour.

He'd only given up when the lights had gone out for the night.

He remembered every detail of how it had ended.

But he never knew why.

And that was what he wanted to know. That was what he'd come so far to find out.

That was the question he needed to have answered.

Why had she broken his heart?

It wasn't just the whim of a sad old fool. It was important that he knew. Because she'd broken his heart in such a way that it never quite fitted together again. Not properly. Not so's he could fall in love again. Properly.

Why?

And in the end he realised he owed it to himself to find out. He owed it to himself, and to the women he had almost loved.

And to his broken heart.

A voice broke into the sombre trance his memories had induced. It shattered the spell.

'Can I help you?' A woman with a child in her arms had opened the front door. 'You've been staring at the house for a long time. Did you want something?'

John-Joseph came to the gate.

'I'm looking for someone who lived here once,' he said. 'The Clark family. Abby Clark in particular.'

'I'm sorry,' the friendly mum said. 'I've never heard of them. We bought the house two years ago, from a young couple who separated. Before them, it was a single man. A bachelor. Who died.

'That's all I know.'

'Well, thank you anyway…' and he went on his way.

But where to?

It seemed he'd reached the final dead-end in his search.

He suddenly wondered what JonJo would

do. Not the jaded, world weary John-Joseph. But the young, energetic, in-love-with-life JonJo.

What would he do now?

That was an easy one to answer. JonJo would do what he always did, whenever he was down, dispirited, deflated. And even when he wasn't. Especially when he wasn't.

JonJo would go to The Cavern.

For the first time in his life JonJo got there late. The Wednesday after he first met Abby, he arrived at The Cavern in the nick of time, slipping inside only moments before it became physically impossible to pack another human body into the crowded underground club.

He struggled through the good-natured mob inside until he saw Dillon waving through the blue haze of cigarette smoke.

'JonJo, where have you been? For a minute we thought you weren't comin'!'

'Sorry, Dill! I had somethin' to do! I'm here now!'

Bomber wasn't satisfied. 'Not before time,' he complained. 'D'you know how hard it's been keepin' your place? You should see the Teddies I've had to fight off to keep hold of that seat!'

'It's true, JonJo,' Dill said. 'He's just risked life an' limb to see off a couple of right bruisers!'

'Thanks, Bomber.'

But Dill was laughing. 'Two of the roughest-lookin' girls I've ever seen!'

'Now, now, don't worry, Dill,' Bomber said reassuringly. 'I sent them both packin'. We won't be seein' that pair again.'

'I don't know about that, Bomb.' Dill nudged him. 'I got their phone numbers!'

'Good lad! Are we desperate or what!?'

The two friends laughed and the banter went on. Colin moved to let JonJo have one of the hard wooden chairs.

'Did you get into town, then?' he asked him. 'Did you get the new single?'

'I did, Col. And it's smashin'! Played it non-stop all Saturday night!'

'Can I borrow it then?'

'Er, no. Sorry, you can't. I don't have it no more.'

The others looked at him suspiciously.

'How's that?'

'I gave it to someone. That's where I was tonight. Droppin' it off.'

'You gave it to someone?' Colin gasped. 'Like who?'

JonJo tried to shrug dismissively, and failed. 'A girl. Just a girl. You don't know her.'

'A girl. Uh-oh! This sounds dangerous, boys,' Dill declared. 'You're not gonna start missin' our Wednesday nights are you, JonJo?'

'Don't be soft! 'Course I'm not! I love Wednesdays here more than anythin'!'

'Well…' JonJo reconsidered '…almost anythin'. Besides, who needs a single? We've got the real thing!'

Conversation suddenly became impossible. Four figures in white shirts, black ties and waistcoats appeared on the stage.

The crowd went wild as the first ear-splitting chords bounced off the bare brick walls of the arches and tunnels.

'Love, love me do.

You know I love you...'

Yeah, who needs a single, JonJo thought. I've got the real thing!

John-Joseph came out of the Beatles Exhibition feeling more than just a little subdued.

He climbed the stairs from the basement beneath what was now a red-brick office block and shopping arcade and stood for some moments blinking uncontrollably in the afternoon sunshine.

But it wasn't the contrast of darkness to daylight that suddenly made his eyes water. And it wasn't the tang of any freshly squeezed memories either.

If anything, it was the absence of such memories that hastened the tears.

He was surprised, and disappointed, at the lack of emotion he'd felt in the exhibition.

Especially in The Cavern itself.

It was nobody's fault. They had done a remarkable job. The Cavern was there. Rebuilt meticulously in every detail, using, if he remembered correctly, thousands of bricks from the original club. Cleverly recreating the sounds and smells and atmosphere of the place, it was exactly as he remembered it. And yet nothing like it at all!

Incredibly accurate as it was, for him, there was something missing.

JonJo was missing. JonJo and the thousands like him, fresh souls, new to life and the ways of the world, still raw but with hearts full of dreams and their whole lives unguessed-at before them.

How could anyone recreate that 40 years later?

A second-hand story, no matter how brilliantly told, must remain second-hand.

As with all the best things in life, you had to be there.

Well, John-Joseph Delaney had been there. As a different person perhaps, but he'd been there. With his hopes and dreams unspoiled – with his precious Bold Street Boys, and with his Abby.

His tears were a simple acknowledgement that he could never go there again.

He hadn't been walking long when suddenly, and almost uniquely for him, he felt utterly wearied.

His head hurt. His arms and legs ached. The jet-lag he had fought against so stubbornly was taking its toll.

He desperately needed a seat.

Ahead of him a bus was standing at the kerb, one of those City of Liverpool jump-on jump-off, open-air tour buses.

Stagger-on stagger-off might be more accurate, he thought, as he dragged himself up the narrow, curving steps.

On the upper deck he fell into a seat with a gasp of relief.

As the bus moved off, John-Joseph relaxed and gave himself up to the experience. His tiredness was quickly replaced with a pleasant feeling of anticipation. The thought of Liverpool unfolding before him gave him a sense of being re-introduced to an old friend...

Then suddenly Abby was there on the pavement below. He saw her face, upturned towards him for a moment as she swept past in a rush of youthful exuberance.

But in seconds she was swallowed by the entrance to a shopping mall. She vanished, leaving him rooted to his seat, his senses reeling, his mind tumbling before a dizzy wave of déjà vu!

Pulling himself from his seat he stumbled to the back of the bus. He hurtled down the steps yelling, 'Stop! Stop the bus!' to the alarm of passengers, driver, and tour guide alike.

Even so, too many precious seconds were lost before the bus pulled over and he could safely jump to the ground.

His eyes scoured the street as he ran, but she was gone.

He searched the mall, looking in every

shop he passed, but she was nowhere to be seen. There were any number of ways she could have gone, too many other doors she could have left by.

In the moments it had taken the bus to stop she had disappeared.

But so had his exhaustion. Even gasping for breath as he was, heart thumping, blood racing, John-Joseph felt renewed. He felt invigorated and insanely optimistic.

It had been her face!

Abby's face!

Incredibly, as young as she had ever been. Just 17. As if the years had never touched her, as if the passage of time had had no power over her.

It had been no mere likeness, not simply an uncanny resemblance or stunning similarity. This had been Abby's face, with Abby's soul behind it, shaping it, giving it life and personality. Abby's personality, that he knew as well as he knew his own.

Whoever she was; daughter, grand-daughter, or the impossible reincarnation of

Abby herself, he knew for certain now that she was here. Still within Liverpool. Still within reach.

Something of JonJo had taken him to The Cavern today – and, in turn, to the open-topped bus that he'd been on. And something of Abby, that one glimpse of her face, had given him the encouragement he needed, the strength to continue his search.

Coming to The Cavern had given him hope after all.

It always had...

CHAPTER TWO

John-Joseph haunted the mall for days.

The large indoor precinct of expensive shops and eating places was the only link he had to his mystery girl. This girl who was the absolute image of Abby. At least, Abby as she had been 40 years ago.

Since the moment he had seen her, that first and only time, dashing across the road in front of his open-topped bus and disappearing through the doors of the mall, one thought had been ever-present in his mind.

She came here before, she might come here again.

So he rose each day, breakfasted quickly, and left the hotel often before it was even fully daylight.

Every day he was first at the mall, the security guards eyeing him suspiciously as they unlocked the doors. And each evening he was last to leave as, one by one, the lights went out and the shutters came down in the fashionable stores.

At first, his plan was to find a vantage point close to where he'd seen the girl and to wait there, for however long it took.

He chose a bench just inside the main doors and sat in hope. For hours on end he remained at his post, alert and focused, as the first early trickle of individuals turned into a day-long flow of customers and consumers.

John-Joseph watched them come and go, his eyes flicking rapidly from face to face, dismissing those who were clearly nothing like her, lingering instead on figures and faces that bore even the slightest resemblance to the girl he was looking for.

All life was here in the mall.

He saw middle-aged couples arm in arm and harassed young mums in their droves. Teenage girls acting cool; teenage boys acting tough to impress them. Elderly women window-shopping, elderly men complaining, and fed-up shop assistants continually slipping outside for a smoke.

Once, a child ran past pursued by a woman too old to be its mother. She caught up with the toddler and gave it a serious ticking off; then immediately countered the scolding with sweets, and the harshness of her voice with a kiss and a hug.

John-Joseph smiled.

A grandmother's discipline.

It took him back.

'JonJo! Where are you, JonJo?'

'What is it, Gran? I'm in a rush! The boys'll be here soon!'

'The Bold Street Boys? Don't make me laugh! Bunch o' kids just out o' nappies tryin' to look older than they are!'

'Did you want somethin', Gran? Or could you shut the bathroom door and insult me through it? I'm tryin' to shave!'

'Shave! That fluff you've got doesn't need shavin'! A good wash'll have it off!'

'Gran–!'

JonJo's mum had died when he was small. His dad was in 'the Merch' – The Merchant Navy. He hadn't been home in 18 months, and that had just been overnight. It was almost two years since JonJo had spent a weekend with the man.

The occasional note, or a packet of bubblegum wrapped in a ten dollar bill, was all JonJo had by way of parental guidance.

He lived with his Irish gran, a leathery 76-year-old, who gave him three times the love and twice the grief a boy could ever want.

His brother, Frankie, older by 15 years, was doing well in business and never came through the door without presents or food.

JonJo idolised his brother. In a city full of wide boys and hard men Frankie was a bit of both and a lot more besides. JonJo was devoted to him.

He once asked what line of 'business' his brother was in. Frankie shrugged his shoulders and looked away. He caught Gran's troubled expression and said, 'Insurance, our kid. Just insurance.'

JonJo had never been encouraged to ask again.

'I want to know where you're goin' tonight! While you're livin' in my house I've a right to know!' His gran was determined.

'You ask the same thing every Wednesday, Gran! And every Wednesday I tell you, I'm goin' to The Cavern!'

'The Cavern! Pah! What's that I'd like to know? A hole in the ground with no heatin'? I don't know what you see in it!'

They had this conversation every week. As

regular as *Dr Finlay's Casebook* on the telly. And as comforting.

'The Beatles, Gran! That's what I see in it! The Beatles!'

'Who're they when they're at home?'

'Only the biggest thing to hit this city since, well, since the Luftwaffe probably!'

'I've never heard of them!'

'That's hardly surprisin', is it? You've not heard of anythin' post-Ivor Novello! But you will, Gran! Believe me, you will!'

He was right. Before long the whole world had heard of The Beatles. Even his gran.

Of course, she still preferred Ivor Novello.

Taken aback by these echoes of yesterday, John-Joseph got to his feet and stretched his legs. Stiffly, he walked around the bench, keeping his wits about him, not letting his concentration slip, in case Abby should choose that moment to slip past him unobserved.

He wasn't deluding himself. He was clutching at straws. But he was doing it simply because he didn't know what else to do.

She came here before, she might come here again.

He was 59 years old. A self-made man. Successful in business, with a reputation for unclouded commonsense. Determined, fiercely pragmatic. And down-to-earth.

Yet here he was now unashamedly hoping for a miracle.

As each day passed with no success, irrational fears began to gnaw.

He worried he was doing the wrong thing. He became convinced that while he sat at one entrance, the girl he sought passed gaily through another.

Afraid of arriving just too late, and leaving just too early, he obsessed that he was missing her by minutes, or seconds, or inches.

On the ground floor he felt sure she was directly overhead on the floor above, but when he hurried to the escalator he knew for certain that she was passing the very bench he'd just vacated.

In the end he became so agitated he

attracted the attention of the police. Two constables inquired off-handedly if he needed any help.

Embarrassed, John-Joseph leaned against a litter bin and caught his breath.

'I'm fine, thank you, officers. Fine,' he said. 'I thought I saw someone I knew, that's all.

'I was mistaken!'

Only when the police moved on, reassured by his explanation and respectable appearance, did John-Joseph come to realise that in many ways it wasn't he who had undertaken this incredible vigil at all.

It was the ghost of JonJo, haunting the busy mall day after day.

It was JonJo, his reckless, more idealistic younger self, who, as long as ago as 1962, had shown such patience where his passions were involved.

Life had never been better for JonJo. He had the kind of friends that only the young can have. Friends with an unspoken bond between them. A bond of teenage intensity they were embarrassed to talk about.

Once-in-a-lifetime friends.

The kind you never fully appreciate until they're gone.

He had The Beatles, who showed the world that ordinary blokes could do extra-ordinary things; four Liverpool lads who took music away from the mums and dads and gave it to the kids.

Like Bill Haley had done. Like Elvis had done. But not in America. Here! They'd done it here in his own back yard!

A once-in-a-lifetime group.

The kind you never fully appreciate until it's gone.

And he had Abby, who took this special life and made it even more special. The only girl he'd kissed for anything other than a laugh. The only one he'd loved as much as his friends, and as much as The Beatles.

A once-in-a-lifetime love.

The kind you never ever forget.

They'd been together a month, long enough for her to know that beneath his typical teenage recklessness, JonJo had a sweet, wide-eyed sincerity. An honesty that was anything but typical.

It was unique. Uniquely JonJo.

'Trust me, Abby, it'll live in your head – like – for ever!'

He was talking about The Beatles.

Christmas was coming, and so was the most incredible night in the history of The Cavern.

'An all-nighter?' Abby said doubtfully. 'An all-night gig?'

'Till dawn!' JonJo beamed. 'Can you imagine how great that will be?'

Abby could. But it didn't make any difference.

'JonJo,' she said gently, 'I can't spend a night at The Cavern. My folks won't hear of it!'

'What?'

'My dad! He won't let me!'

JonJo looked as if he couldn't grasp the meaning of her words. He couldn't believe that anyone's dad would stop them seeing

The Beatles.

'Would it help if I had a word with him?' he said.

'Oh, yeah,' Abby said, suddenly amused. 'Tell him I won't just be stayin' out all night – I'll be stayin' out all night with my boy-friend!

'That'll do it.' She laughed.

She stopped when she saw how hurt he was – and how desperately disappointed.

'Soft lad,' she said, squeezing his hand. 'It's all right. I'll survive. You go. Enjoy the gig. Then tell me about it. Tell me all about it in your funny, amazin' way. That'll be even more fantastic than seein' it for myself.'

He gave in. 'But it won't be the same without you, Abby.'

And he meant it.

JonJo queued outside The Cavern for a week. He camped-out alone, though sometimes Colin skipped art school, too, to keep him company.

Bomber and Dillon turned up when they

could, on their lunch breaks from work.

In the evenings, Abby brought sandwiches and they picnicked on the pavement of Matthew Street.

By Saturday, the pavements were crammed with hundreds and hundreds of fans. Some had been there for days. But in his thick donkey jacket and woolly hat, with his thermal underwear and sleeping bag, JonJo was the local hero.

He'd been there all week.

And it was worth every minute when Abby appeared that night, pushing her way through the crowded Cavern to the extra seat he had kept – just in case.

In scarlet hip huggers with her hair tied back he thought she was the most wonderful thing he had ever seen in his life.

'How on earth–?' He was almost speechless. 'How can–?'

'I told my dad I was spendin' the night at Susan's!'

Susan was Abby's older cousin, who had brought her to The Cavern on the night

46

when she and JonJo first saw each other. She could be trusted absolutely. And that was important.

'I've never lied to my dad before,' Abby said seriously. 'Not once.'

'Are you sure about this?' JonJo asked.

'I am,' she said. 'He won't suspect a thing. He'll never know.'

But JonJo knew, he knew exactly what she'd done for him.

And that night when The Beatles played, they made it all worthwhile. They changed the lives of a thousand people, set their hearts and dreams on fire, and swept away every niggling trace of fear and doubt from Abby's mind.

That night, thanks to JonJo's impossible patience, the Bold Street Boys and Abby had the prime position, right at the front, close enough to see the sweat on Ringo's forehead and the sparkle in Paul's eyes.

And that night, when Abby reached out a hand and touched the toe of his boot, John Lennon smiled and looked down at her, an expression of pure joy on his exquisite young face.

John Lennon's face was looking up at him now. No longer exquisitely young and full of joy, but long-haired, bearded, eyes melancholy and knowing behind their wire-rimmed spectacles, drawn in chalk on the paving stones of a city centre square not far from the mall.

John-Joseph was late. He'd overslept and the day had begun without him.

Hurrying to the shopping mall, he'd reached a pedestrian crossing and stood there waiting for the stream of traffic to stop and let him cross.

Shuffling his feet impatiently, annoyed beyond belief by the delay, he'd suddenly become aware of music in the air. And the words to one of his favourite Beatles' songs.

Yesterday, love was such an easy game to play. Now I need a place to hide away.

Behind him, easily overlooked on the busy street, a pedestrian walkway led between two stores. John-Joseph followed it to a hidden square of open-air cafés and smaller, slightly more bohemian shops.

People were drinking coffee; kids were rollerblading; a man old enough to know better was playing a guitar.

On the ground, beside a row of slender trees, was the amazing likeness of a long-dead Beatle. And kneeling beside the picture, chalk in hand, was the very girl he had been looking for.

John-Joseph's world stopped for a moment. 'Yesterday' became a whisper at the edges of his mind. And John Lennon seemed to smile.

She tossed her hair back and lifted her head. And there it was, that face. That perfect face. With Abby's eyes, and Abby's lips, and the full soft curve of Abby's cheek.

Unfortunately, Abby's nose was pierced on one side by a little silver ring, and the unexpectedness of such a thing completely took John-Joseph's breath away.

It was a shocking reminder, if he needed

one, that this girl wasn't Abby, couldn't possibly be, however much her looks might lie.

'People usually stare at the picture,' she said. 'Not at me!'

'I – yes – I'm sorry!' John-Joseph stammered an apology. 'But you look very much like someone I used to know.

'Is it possible your mother's name is Abby?'

Dropping her chalk the girl jumped to her feet. Her expression, so friendly a moment ago, was glowering and deeply suspicious.

'Abby Greenwood! As if you didn't know!'

'I'm sorry–?'

'You know fine well who my mother is! She sent you, didn't she? To find me! With another lecture, another speech! Well, I'm not interested!

'Go back and tell her that, will you!'

John-Joseph was utterly taken aback.

'I don't understand–!'

'But I do,' the girl bleated. 'I understand she won't be satisfied until I'm miserable! As miserable as she is!'

She was on her knees again, scrabbling on the ground to gather up her few possessions. A little tin of coloured chalks, a duster, and the photograph of Lennon she'd been copying.

Pushing them into a backpack she got to her feet.

'Why can't she leave me alone?' she said. 'Why can't she just let me be happy?'

'I don't know what you mean, ' John-Joseph was bewildered. 'I'm a friend of your mum's, but an old friend! I haven't seen her in years! I was hoping you could give me an address where I might find her!'

The girl clearly wasn't convinced.

'Is that the truth?' she said. 'Why should I believe you?'

'It's true! I promise you! I knew your mum well! Very well!' John-Joseph was beginning to babble as an alarming surge of desperation rose inside him. He took hold of her shoulders.

'Abby – Abby Clark she was then – went to the Collegiate. The Grammar School!

She loves dancing, and The Beatles–'

And me, he almost said, but didn't. He managed to stop himself in time. The girl was looking at him warily enough as it was.

'Are you all right, 'Chelle? Who's this? Who's the old guy?' Voice shrill and alarmed, a teenage boy hurried towards them across the square.

Lost in the folds of an outsized sweatshirt, with shapeless baggy trousers and a baseball cap turned backwards, he lunged at them like an unmade bed, thrusting himself between John-Joseph and the girl.

'Back off, man!' he bridled.

'He says he's a friend of my mum's!' the girl said.

That only seemed to anger the boy more.

'Why can't you people just leave us alone? We're cool together!'

If John-Joseph hadn't been so rattled, it would have struck a nostalgic chord in him, this mix of American slang and outright scouse.

But he was shaken by the boy ranting in

his face.

The girl's aggression, on the other hand, had completely evaporated, to be replaced by very obvious concern. Genuinely scared, she grabbed the boy's arm and tried to pull him away.

'Leave him, Zack, he's not worth it!' Half-turning towards John-Joseph, she pleaded, 'Get out of here, Mister! Please! Just go!'

Reluctantly, the boy allowed himself to be ushered away, dragging his feet, stumbling backwards, never taking his eyes from John-Joseph's face.

But John-Joseph had come too far and tried too hard to find this girl. He wasn't about to let her disappear now.

'I'm sorry,' he insisted, 'you've got it all wrong!'

He moved after them, but the young boy stepped around the girl and seemed to square his shoulders for a fight, John-Joseph stopped abruptly, blinking nervously.

'At least give me a chance to explain!' he appealed. 'Talk about it.' But the girl was hustling her boyfriend away again.

'My name's Delaney!' he shouted after them, in a desperate attempt to save the day. 'I'm staying at The Marriot! The Marriot Hotel, Queens Square!'

'Don't hold your breath!' the boy jeered. 'You'll die waitin'!'

John-Joseph already felt as if a part of him had died. The part that clung to the hope of seeing Abby again.

Troubled by the confrontation; shaken by the threat of violence; he sat in the square for a while to calm himself.

Then, deeply discouraged, he dropped some coins into the busker's cap and grudgingly made his way back to his hotel.

He spent the rest of the day, and all of the next, hanging around the hotel in case the girl came looking for him.

He didn't really expect it and was desperately afraid he'd never see her again.

He'd never been much good at killing time. Inactivity depressed him, and a feeling of helplessness gripped him now. A feeling that even a phone call to Australia couldn't dispel.

He called his secretary in the middle of the day, forgetting that, for her, it was the middle of the night.

'What if I've scared her off, Roddy? What if she doesn't come? What do I do then?'

Alone, in the darkness, on the other side of the world, his former secretary clung to the phone, taking comfort in his voice if not in his words.

'It was a miracle I found her in the first place. As if, somehow, I was being led to her … guided towards her by memories of The Cavern, and The Beatles, and their music.'

She had never heard him speak like this before. He hardly sounded like the man she'd known – and loved – for such a very long time.

These last 17 years had been spent seeing to his every need, smoothing the way ahead for him, taking care of him in both his professional and personal life.

Through difficult times and dazzling

triumphs; through two broken engagements – she had been his support, his counsel, his touchstone of stability and strength.

And she'd never given him the slightest indication of how much it had meant to her. Or how much it had cost her.

Nor did she now. She listened, sympathetically, and she didn't let on that the more he talked the farther away he seemed.

'It's almost as if I was meant to find her, Roddy.'

She listened and, as she'd always done, told him what he needed to hear.

'Perhaps you were – and if that's the case, I'm sure she'll come. Don't you believe in destiny? In fate?'

It was a question he'd been asking himself a lot recently.

'I'll let you know,' he said. 'If I ever see her again!'

A few minutes later, coming downstairs for lunch, he found the young girl waiting at Reception.

Sprawled across an armchair in the same worn-out trainers and fraying jeans she looked completely out-of-place in the plush hotel. Completely out-of-place, and completely at ease. More at ease, in fact, that John-Joseph sometimes felt in these five-star surroundings.

When she saw him, she got to her feet and smiled sheepishly.

'I owe you an apology for the other day,' she said. 'You must've thought we were a right pair of nutters!'

'Not at all,' he said politely, shrugging it off, trying to conceal his excitement over the fact that she was here.

'Zack wouldn't have hurt you,' she continued.

'And yet,' he said, with a knowing smile, 'you felt the need to protect me.'

The girl looked taken aback and laughed out loud!

'I wasn't protectin' you!' she said. 'I was protectin him! Zack's no fighter. I wanted to get him away in case you hurt him!

'But he was, like, totally over-the-top, and I'm sorry.'

John-Joseph smiled at her warmly.

'Look, I don't know anything about your issues with your mum,' he said. 'But I would like to see her again, if you'll give me an address.'

'How long has it been since you've seen her?'

'Forty years.'

The girl laughed again, good-naturedly.

'You don't believe in rushin' things, do you? If you want, I'll take you there. I suppose it's the least I can do.'

John-Joseph felt the weight of the last few days lift from his shoulders. He felt the terrible hopelessness drain from his pores and in its place came a rush of pure relief.

Now he could afford to be calm. He could take the time to savour the thought that soon he would be seeing Abby again.

'Why don't we eat first?' he suggested.

'In there?' the girl said in disbelief, looking towards the fancy dining-room.

'Why not?'

She looked at John-Joseph and stuck out her chin, and a spark of devilment seemed to come into her eyes.

'Why not?' she agreed, tickled pink.

With a little flourish, John-Joseph stepped aside to let her pass. She looked at him as if he was outrageously old-fashioned. Then she laughed again.

'What is it?' he asked.

She shook her head. 'Just wonderin'. How long's it been since anyone took you home to meet their mum?'

Abby was devoted to her father. When she spoke of him it was always with a childlike glow, her voice a blend of pride and admiration.

She loved her mum, too, but was, in no uncertain terms, her daddy's girl.

'He's a great dad, JonJo. A great man, and a great policeman!'

JonJo smiled wryly and raised his eyebrows fleetingly. It had taken him the best

59

part of a month to get used to the idea that he was dating a policeman's daughter!

'I love and adore him,' Abby said unequivocally. 'And you will, too.'

'Yeah, well, we'll see about that,' JonJo said as he watched her put the key in her front door. 'I love and adore his daughter. That's enough to be goin' on with!'

Inside the suburban semi-detached the family was waiting. They stood up as the teenagers entered the room. Abby's parents, and another woman with an ill-advised home perm.

Already nervous, Abby gave a startled little cough.

'Hello, Aunt Dora.' She glanced at JonJo. 'Aunt Dora, JonJo. Susan's mum.'

Already terror-stricken, JonJo felt his spinal column turn to water.

'Susan?'

'Susan!' Abby's father said, looking directly at his daughter. 'With whom you did NOT spend the night last Saturday!'

He turned his gaze on JonJo, who quivered

like a rabbit caught in the headlights of a truck, and took the boy's hand in a grip he could have used for crushing walnuts.

'Am I to assume that this is the person with whom you did!'

JonJo almost expected the man to read him his rights.

Over lunch, John-Joseph came to realise how much he liked the girl. She was 17 years old and called Michelle.

Michelle, ma belle!

Could that possibly be what lay behind the name?

She was pretty, she was intelligent and she was spunky. Just like her mother – or at least – just like he remembered her mother.

But there were differences between them. Many, and marked.

'Isn't it a little irresponsible, and dangerous,' John-Joseph said, 'going off with a stranger like this? You don't know anything about me.'

Michelle gave him a worldly smile and

shook her head. 'I can usually spot the weirdos,' she said. 'Besides, you remind me a bit of my dad...'

She had a car, a smart little Mini Cooper. As she drove them through the Mersey Tunnel heading towards Prenton, Wirral, she pushed a tape into the dashboard player and turned up the volume.

Suddenly, without warning, what sounded like a stream of profanity, set to an unrelenting beat that you couldn't call music, assaulted John-Joseph's ears and set his teeth on edge.

Nothing at all like the music of JonJo's day. Songs with tunes, full of innocence and happiness, about holding hands and falling in love.

Sure, there was pain and suffering, usually the pain of a broken heart, but a pain that was tempered by hope and the chance of falling in love again.

Not the unremitting gloom of today's visionaries.

Whatever happened to music that made

you glad to be a teenager? Was it really over 40 years ago? It seemed like yesterday.

Michelle glanced sideways trying to gauge what he thought of the tape.

'D'you know who that is?' she said. 'That's Zack. My Zack.' And she said it with unmistakable pride. 'He's good.'

Unable to think of an appropriate response John-Joseph remained silent. He looked out the window and tried to block the music from his mind.

Now that Abby was close, closer than she'd been for many years, he was feeling nervous and a good deal unsure of himself.

What on earth was he going to say to her? What was she going to think, seeing him again after all this time? What was her husband going to think?

As it happened, though, that wasn't to be an issue.

'Mum and Dad are a long time divorced,' Michelle said. 'My dad's remarried. I lived with him until I moved in with Zack.

'The car belongs to my stepmum but I

borrow it once in a while.'

Her voice faltered imperceptibly. 'I've not seen my own mum for months.'

'Why not?'

The girl shrugged carelessly and pulled a face. Her voice was controlled again, jokey and light. John-Joseph didn't know her well enough to identify what deeper emotions, if any, might be hidden underneath.

'Her and Zack don't get on. She's never liked any of my boyfriends, but she especially seems to have it in for Zack!

'I don't know why!'

Perhaps, John-Joseph thought, she'd heard him sing.

John-Joseph's hand was shaking as he opened the door of the car.

Michelle had brought them to an elegant and very expensive property on Mount Wood Road in Prenton.

He looked at the house admiringly with a knowledgeable eye. If this was Abby's she had done well for herself. Very well.

'It's my sister's house,' Michelle said, as if reading his mind. 'My brother-in-law's worth a bundle. He's something to do with computers!'

'Like a programmer?' John-Joseph asked.

'Like a mouse!' said the girl. And she grinned.

It was a fair walk up the drive to the porch and John-Joseph grew more tense with every step. He braced himself and cleared his throat as the young girl rang the bell.

The door opened at last to reveal an older incarnation of Michelle, a woman in her thirties, immaculately dressed and impeccably poised.

But her self-assurance slipped at the sight of her sister, and it positively shook when she saw John-Joseph. It seemed to him that she had been expecting someone else.

'Michelle, what are you doing here?' she said abruptly. 'And who..?' Then, as if she realised how rude that must have sounded, 'I mean, this is a surprise. What can I do for you?'

'I've come to see Mum,' the girl said, 'if it's all right with you.'

It didn't seem to be.

'Good grief, Michelle! You might have phoned!'

'I didn't know I needed an appointment, Eleanor!'

Eleanor? John-Joseph clicked his tongue.

Eleanor Rigby,

Picks up the rice in the church where a wedding has been...

Two Beatles songs. Two names. Michelle and Eleanor. It had to be deliberate.

Eleanor's exasperation didn't seem to be deliberate. It came across as perfectly spontaneous and natural.

'Of course you don't need an appointment,' she said. 'You're family.'

But it was said in such a way as to underline the fact that John-Joseph was not.

'This is John-Joseph Delaney,' Michelle said, at last. 'He used to go out with Mum.'

It sounded pathetic.

Over the years, John-Joseph had almost

never talked about Abby. To put their love into words was to devalue it. It made people believe they understood something they never could understand.

It made a special love seem commonplace.

Eleanor certainly thought so. Her displeasure was clear.

'I don't believe you, sometimes,' she groaned disparagingly, at the same time leading Michelle and John-Joseph inside.

'How could you think of bringing him here at a time like this?'

The criticism stung her younger sister. Tears sprang into her eyes and her voice was strained. 'I thought it might help!'

'You fool, Michelle! You absolute fool!'

John-Joseph stood self-consciously, out of things.

He felt like an intruder, an alien, completely and utterly ignorant of the details and even the language that went to make up the lives of these people.

Eleanor noticed his discomfort and took pity on him. She apologised for seeming to exclude him.

'My mother isn't here right now,' she said. 'This is one of the days she has to stay in hospital.'

Michelle immediately flinched and shied away.

It was almost as if her sister's words had the power to do her actual physical harm.

John-Joseph watched as the young girl shook her head in sudden anguish.

His mouth went dry.

'Is Abby unwell then?' he asked tentatively.

Eleanor spoke with the voice of someone used to putting terrible news into words.

'More than unwell. I'm sorry, Mr Delaney, but my sister should have told you. Our mother is dying.'

CHAPTER THREE

'I'm sorry, Mr Delaney, but my sister should have told you. Our mother is dying.'

John-Joseph felt himself go cold – an icy chill was radiating from somewhere deep, expelling every ounce of warmth from his body.

Michelle gave a little cry of anguish and ran from the room, desperately trying to suppress a flow of sobs.

Seconds later the front door slammed so violently it seemed to shake the house.

Alarmed, John-Joseph felt he should go after her but he found himself quite unable to move. He was still struggling to take in the news that Eleanor had delivered so calmly and in such a controlled tone of voice.

Eleanor herself hadn't moved an inch. She just stood there, looking down at the carpet between them.

'My mother has secondary cancer,' she said, finally breaking their long silence. 'They're treating her, but I don't think … I don't think anyone's holding out much hope. Michelle can't – or won't – accept it.'

'She's very young,' John-Joseph observed.

'Nonetheless, we can't ignore the painful facts of life.'

Looking at the older sister; at the set of her mouth, the tightness of her jaw, the almost unbearable tension in the muscles of her throat; John-Joseph saw the strain she was under, and reflected that everyone locks out grief in their own individual way.

Or locks it in.

The front door opened again and he assumed that Michelle had come back, having somehow managed to rally her rapidly crumbling defences.

Instead, a ghost from his past suddenly appeared in a slim flurry of woollen coat-tails. Throwing off her gloves and scarf, and throwing out an endless stream of questions,

Abby swept into the house full of spirit and fire.

'Ellie! Ellie, where are you? Was that Michelle's car? Was she here? We saw a car pull away and I thought – was it her? Was it 'Chelle?'

She didn't appear as ill as she must have been.

She was thin, but not painfully so. She was pale, but not alarmingly.

The freshness of the day had even put colour in her cheeks.

The thought of seeing her youngest daughter had given a sparkle to her eyes.

But the sight of the man in front of her drew her up suddenly, and froze the flow of questions on her lips.

She stared at John-Joseph and saw someone else entirely.

'JonJo?'

She spoke the name that no-one in the world used now. Then spoke it again.

'JonJo? Good grief! JonJo!'

She crossed the room in an impulsive whirl,

and threw her arms around him. They clung to each other so tightly and for such a long time that her daughter's astonished husband had closed the front door and removed his coat, and his wife had gone to the kitchen to make coffee for them all, before John-Joseph took a breath and found his voice and squeezed out a trembling, 'Hello.'

Abby didn't want coffee. Despite Eleanor's protest, she wanted to go for a walk.

'But you always rest after your treatment,' her daughter insisted. 'You're tired, Mum. You need to sleep.'

'How could I sleep with JonJo here?' Her eyes wide as Heaven, never left his face.

'The doctor says you mustn't overdo things. You should lie down.'

'Eleanor. Please. Don't fuss,' Abby said the words gently, but her daughter was still hurt by them. Eleanor folded her arms across her chest and turned her head away.

'We won't be long,' her mother promised. 'And we can all have coffee as soon as we get back.'

'It's cold out,' Eleanor said stubbornly. 'Where's your scarf? At least wrap up well...'

Retrieving Abby's scarf and gloves, she helped her mother put them on.

'Thanks, "Mum",' Abby said, humbly, and the women smiled at each other with affection, masking whatever regret they might have felt.

Walking away from the house, John-Joseph had an overwhelming desire to hold Abby's hand. But he resisted, not wanting to presume anything.

'I feel guilty,' he confessed, 'taking you out if you should be resting!'

'Don't be ridiculous,' Abby said. 'Seeing you like this is more of a tonic than any amount of rest!

'What are you doing here? How did you get here? Why – after all this time–?' She shook her head excitedly, an incredulous look on her face. She eventually shrugged off the hundreds of questions she had and settled for one.

'How on earth did you find me?'

So, as they walked, they talked, not about resting or illness or loss. Rather, they talked about life. John-Joseph's life.

'I've lived in Australia,' he said, 'for a long time now. I've done pretty well for myself. I took early retirement a few months ago, and somebody said quite naturally, "what are you going to do now?"

'I realised, to my complete surprise, that what I *most* wanted to do, was look for you...

'But tracing you proved to be almost impossible. So I came over myself, and, miraculously, caught sight of Michelle from the top of a bus.'

'It sounds unbelievably simple.' Abby laughed.

'Not simple,' said John-Joseph, 'just un-believable. It took The Cavern, John Lennon, and an old Beatles song, to find her!' And he added, 'She's lovely, Abby. It's incredible how much she looks like you.'

Abby's hair, cut short and expertly styled to disguise its thinness, only emphasised the striking similarity between herself and Michelle.

She sighed from the depths of a mother's heart.

'Things aren't good between us right now,' she confessed. 'We've had a lot of problems. Mostly over her choice of boyfriends. Partly over her dad and I divorcing.

'She, quite rightly, blames me for that.'

For the first time she faltered, sounding a little self-conscious. She carried on quickly, 'Now she's using it all as an excuse for staying away. She can't come to terms with my illness, you see. She's in complete denial.

'Today's the first day she's been to the house in months. I'm so desperately sorry I missed her.'

She slipped into a melancholy silence, but just for a moment.

'Do you recognise where we are?' she asked.

John-Joseph looked about. 'It's Prenton Park.' He grinned. 'And we've been here before!'

'For our all-American barbecue,' Abby confirmed.

'When Dillon set his tie on fire—'

'—and Bomber had to eat the hamburgers raw!'

John-Joseph laughed, unspeakably happy to think that she remembered as much as he did.

As they walked into the park, she put her hand in his.

'Well, what do you know about that?' he said. 'It still fits.'

'You won't all fit,' said JonJo's gran.

But they did.

JonJo and Abby; Colin and Bomber and Dillon; and Abby's cousin, Susan, who had begun to hang around with them more and more; squeezed cosily into the old woman's parlour.

The lights were off, the television on, and The Beatles were making their first appearance on Thank Your Lucky Stars! It was their introduction to nationwide TV.

All over the country kids were getting their very first taste of the Merseyside madness the world would come to call Beatlemania.

While Colin and Bomber and Dillon and Susan were whistling and cheering and stamping their feet, JonJo fell silent.

He couldn't explain the feeling that had just come over him.

He couldn't explain it because he didn't understand it. He didn't understand that The Beatles belonged to a lot more people now, and so belonged to him a little less.

Only Abby noticed the change in him.

Despite JonJo and her father getting off on absolutely the wrong foot, the young couple had become inseparable.

They never missed a Wednesday night at The Cavern.

They spent their weekends together, often at JonJo's, playing the first Beatles' album, Please Please Me, again and again. Playing it endlessly, until the grooves were almost worn smooth and JonJo's gran was driven to distraction.

They met in the afternoons at the College of Art. Or he'd wait for her outside the gates of her respectable grammar school.

And all the while her father disapproved.

At the Casbah Coffee Club, Abby summed up the situation.

'He knows I lied about staying out all night at The Cavern. I told him it wasn't your idea. And now he thinks I'm lying to protect you.

'He still doesn't want me to see you. But when I tell him I'm not going to stop, I think I see a glint of admiration in his eye.'

'Unless it's unspeakable outrage.' JonJo grinned.

'I think he's proud of me standing up for what I want...

'Oh, and he says if you lay a hand on me, he'll kill you!'

JonJo almost choked on his frothy coffee.

'Well, that's all right then,' he spluttered, eyes almost popping out of his head. 'As long as he's coming round!'

A few days later, JonJo's eyes almost

popped out of his head again, the first time he saw his brother's flash new car.

It was American. A '57 Cadillac Convertible in ice blue with white-wall tyres, leather seats, and a dazzling chrome trim. It was spectacular!

'One of my clients is American,' said Frankie. 'He had two of them brought over and let me have this one at a knock-down price. Out of gratitude, like.'

JonJo couldn't imagine what someone in the insurance business did to warrant gratitude like that.

Frankie grinned at his little brother's look of wonder.

'Want to take it for a drive?'

'Yeah, right!'

'I'm serious, our kid. Go on. You can have it tonight. Pick up that girlfriend of yours, and those mates. Take them to The Cavern in style for a change.'

'No way, man!' JonJo snorted. 'I couldn't!'

JonJo knew how to drive. Frankie had taught him as soon as he was old enough, in

lieu of an absentee father and countless forgotten birthdays.

'Of course you could! Just put your eyes
back in your head and roll your tongue up
first!'

'Wow! Thanks! Frankie! Thanks! You're
the best, man, no kiddin'! The best!'

'Give over,' said his brother seriously. 'I
can't drive it every minute of the day! You
might as well use it whenever it's free!

'If it bothers you, well, maybe you could
make a few deliveries for me in it.'

'Deliveries?'

Frankie shrugged. 'Yeah. This and that.
Keys to the odd business associate. A
package now and then. Nothin' important.'

'Sure, Frankie. I could do that! No sweat!'

And so it was that, suddenly, the Bold
Street Boys had wheels. So it was that they
travelled in style. Once a month. Sometimes
more. To the beaches at Hoylake and Ains-
dale-at-Sea; to Prenton Park and to Wales;
and to the Promenade, New Brighton,
where The Beatles sometimes played the

Tower Ballroom.

Yet Jonjo never drove to Abby's house to pick her up, and after they'd been out together he didn't take her all the way home to her door.

They both agreed it best that he avoided Abby's father for a while.

It was the only shadow cast on their lives through the brightness of a perfect love.

When they got back from their walk, Michelle's car was parked outside the house again.

Abby was still holding John-Joseph's hand. But now she was leaning against his arm for support.

As they walked, the eagerness in her face had been replaced by tiredness. Her eyes had lost some of their sparkle, but only some, as the initial excitement of finding him there, and the hope of seeing her daughter again, had gradually worn off.

But now at the sight of the car her tiredness seemed to disappear.

She quickened her step and hurried John-Joseph towards the house.

Eleanor and her husband, Tony, were in the day room. As he came into the house John-Joseph overheard their conversation and felt sure that Abby must have done so, too.

'How could 'Chelle bring him here, without even knowing if Mum would be happy to see him?'

'She seemed to be.'

'At least she didn't bring the appalling boyfriend.'

Michelle was in the kitchen, keeping out of her sister's way, apparently just waiting for her mother to come home. Abby went to her and hugged her. The girl responded, awkwardly affectionate, as if holding her emotions at bay. As if she wasn't ready to commit herself just yet.

Abby didn't notice, or pretended not to. She touched the young girl's face, her shoulders, gently tugged the spiky hair, then took her hands and entwined their fingers gently.

It was as though she was trying to hold her

daughter everywhere at once.

Standing in the doorway, watching them together, John-Joseph felt a glow of gratification that he had somehow, inadvertently, helped bring this about.

'It's lovely to see you, Michelle,' Abby beamed. 'Thanks for coming. You'll stay for dinner? I'll make something special.'

'I'll do it,' Eleanor said, appearing suddenly pushing her way past John-Joseph abruptly. Everyone can stay. On condition that you rest now!'

She took her mother's arm to lead her away.

'You're over-tired!'

Abby looked apologetically at John-Joseph. 'You don't mind?'

'Of course not.'

'And you'll stay? You'll both stay?'

Michelle nodded, but somehow made even that seem non-committal.

Abby was satisfied, though, and left the kitchen quickly ahead of Eleanor.

John-Joseph thought there was even a

spring in her step. She didn't appear to be over-tired to him.

Dinner passed in a haze of casual conversation.

They sat round a mahogany table, eating with silver cutlery and sharing wine. The food was rich and exquisitely cooked. Then John-Joseph noted that Abby's was something milky, soft, and bland.

John-Joseph tried hard not to mind the family's presence; tried not to resent the to-and-fro of small talk when he had so many more important things to talk to Abby about.

He knew it was unforgivable of him to feel this way but he couldn't help it.

Michelle sat quietly, unforthcoming, giving her mother only sketchy details of her life.

Then Abby said, 'How's Zack?'

'As if you care!'

'Michelle!' Eleanor was livid, but her sister was unabashed.

'Well, you don't! None of you do! You'd much rather I was with somebody else.'

'I'd much rather you were happy,' Abby said honestly.

'How do you know I'm not?' her daughter replied indignantly.

Abby didn't seem to have an answer. Eleanor didn't seem to think the question needed one.

'Any luck with his music?'

'Not yet.'

'Or his habit?' Eleanor added cruelly.

'That's a horrible thing to say!' Michelle wailed. Eleanor's words had utterly demolished all her barriers. 'Zack doesn't take drugs!' Tears sprang into her eyes and she looked at John-Joseph, desperate for some kind of understanding.

'Zack took some pot at a party once.' She sobbed. 'Just once! 'Cos he was curious! He hasn't done it since and I know he'll never do it again!'

'How do you know?' said Abby gently.

Michelle swallowed hard and spoke with touching simplicity.

'Because I asked him not to.'

85

'Oh, well, then, of course!' Eleanor scoffed, highly sceptical. 'Works miracles, doesn't it, young love?'

'It can,' said Michelle, in a little voice. 'Sometimes.' And she looked at John-Joseph. 'I mean, that's why *you're* here, isn't it?'

It was a statement of such boldness, and so wholly unexpected, that it stopped the conversation in its tracks.

John-Joseph couldn't think of a thing to say.

'That's right,' Tony said suddenly, as if he'd only just found his voice. He was a pleasant, if colourless, man. People often found it easy to forget that he was there. Even when he was speaking.

'How long has it been since the two of you met?'

He looked at John-Joseph, then at Abby, and seemed genuinely interested.

'I mean, when did you last see each other?'

JonJo was inconsolable. The Beatles had just announced their last night at The Cavern.

They'd simply grown too big, too fast.

Suddenly they were huge, and everyone wanted a taste of their music, through more and more records, live tours, and television.

And not just in this country.

Even then, America was waiting.

Everyone, everywhere, wanted a piece of The Beatles, and there wasn't going to be enough left over for The Cavern on Wednesday nights.

Their local fans were devastated. And yet even before The Beatles played their last gig, JonJo had come to realise that nothing lasts for ever.

Not even love.

Not even a first love as wonderful as his and Abby's.

As the months slipped past; as winter melted into spring, and spring bloomed into summer; their feelings deepened, growing not more comfortable but more exhilarating, more exciting.

Everything they did, they did together.

Everything they learned, they taught each other.

Each new experience they shared, each boundary they crossed, each new discovery they made about their love, their hearts, their touching, every door they opened, brought them closer, made them stronger, and reaffirmed what they'd known from the very beginning.

This wasn't just a first love, but a last love, for them both.

Sure of this, they were sure of everything. Absolutely and completely. Enough to accept adversity and even to humour Abby's father.

'It's unbelievable,' she groaned. 'He just never lets up. I'm too young to go steady! You're keeping me from my studies! You're putting my future at risk!

'You are my future, JonJo, can't he see that?'

'If he ever tried to make you choose...?'

'I've already chosen, JonJo. I've chosen you. Nothing in this world could come between us.'

He believed her, of course. Even so, he

was upset. He knew how much her father's approval meant to Abby. He was sorry to think he'd done anything to spoil that.

'It's not you, JonJo,' she told him. 'He'd be like this with any boy. No-one's ever going to be good enough for me!'

But she was wrong. It was JonJo. She just didn't know it yet.

But she was to know it soon.

Instead of gradually coming round, instead of growing to accept JonJo as the couple had expected, her father's disapproval deepened, his antagonism became entrenched.

But still it wasn't enough to spoil their love.

Until Abby changed...

She stopped coming to The Cavern. At first, she said, because she had exams and had to study. Soon she'd be leaving school. She had plans to make, university to think about.

Certainly she was thinking about something. Sometimes, when she was with him, she wasn't quite with him. And when he began to see less of her, even at weekends, JonJo knew something was wrong.

Finally, on the night The Beatles quit The Cavern, she dropped her bombshell.

'Abby? What's up? Why didn't you meet me. We're late! They'll be on stage already!'

He watched her through the quickening gloom of the garden as she came towards the gate, the brightly-lit windows of the house behind her. She wasn't wearing a jacket or coat. Clearly she wasn't going anywhere tonight.

Something was different about her. Her face was different. Her eyes were different. Her voice was barely Abby's voice. It sounded stiff and strange and cold to him.

'I won't be going tonight, JonJo,' she said. 'I won't be going anywhere with you any more. It's over.'

He couldn't make sense of the words. They didn't fit together.

'What's over?'

'Us, JonJo,' she said. 'It's time to call it a day.'

JonJo was baffled. She didn't mean it. She couldn't mean it.

'What are you on about, Abby?' His voice was beginning to fall apart.

'I'll be going away soon. To university.'

'Yeah? So? We've talked about all that. 'We'll manage.'

She shivered and folded her arms in front of her. Shielding herself from the cold perhaps, or steeling herself against something much worse.

'I don't want to manage,' she said. 'Things have changed. I've changed. I don't feel the same about us any more. We're too young to make plans. Too young to be getting so serious.'

'Too young–' In a sudden flash of pain, JonJo thought he understood.

'It's your dad!' he said. 'All those months of slagging us off. He's finally got to you. He's put you up to this!'

'He hasn't.

'This is my decision.'

'I don't believe you! He's forcing you into

this. I want to talk to him.'

He tried to open the gate but Abby put her hands against it. JonJo saw that they were trembling. She looked ill.

'He's not in!' Her voice was abrupt. It didn't belong to Abby. 'It's got nothing to do with him anyway, JonJo. It's what I want.'

'Why, Abby? There's hardly been an angry word between us. You said we'd be together for ever.'

She looked away. 'Too long,' she said. 'Forever's too long.' And then, more kindly, 'It's nothing you've done, JonJo. It's nothing you've said.

'We're young – too young. We fell in love so quickly.'

'And now you're saying, what? You've stopped? You've stopped loving me? Just like that?'

She shrugged her shoulders. 'Feelings change,' she said quietly.

JonJo fought the panic that was rising in his chest and wondered how she could be so calm about it, so matter-of-fact.

'That's it?' He raised his voice in desperation. 'That's all you've got to say to me. Feelings change? It's not enough!'

'It's all there is,' she said. 'Love dies. People move on.'

'Not people like us. Not love like ours. This is rubbish, Abby! I won't let you do it!'

She had slumped a little on to the gate, leaning towards him, almost leaning against him, but suddenly she straightened and stepped away.

'You've no choice,' she said hoarsely. 'Goodbye, JonJo!'

She bent her head and hurried towards the house. Beyond desperation now, JonJo jumped the gate.

'Abby, no! Wait, Abby! Is there something you're not telling me?'

She stopped and looked back at him. 'Yes.'

And then she said it. 'I don't love you any more, JonJo.'

She shook her head sadly, looking him straight in the eye. 'I did, once. But not any more.'

By the time he'd recovered from her words, she had walked stiffly back into the house and closed the door.

He refused to leave. He banged on the door for an hour. He called out and shouted until the neighbours complained. But from Abby's house there didn't come a sound.

Finally, when the lights went out for the night, he left in tears.

For a month his telephone calls went unanswered. His letters were returned. When he waited outside her house the front door remained closed.

A neighbour said that the family was away on holiday, and then that Abby was away at university.

It was to be 40 years before he next set eyes on her.

And he never saw The Beatles play live again.

'Why'd you do it, Abby?' After dinner they had a little time together, while Eleanor and Tony did the clearing up, while Michelle made a phone call, probably to Zack.

Abby and John-Joseph sat in the conservatory. Outside, the darkness of the garden was pierced by tiny lights hung on the trees. Inside, the peace of the moment was pierced by that one, inevitable question.

'Why did we break up. Why did you break us up?'

Abby sighed heavily. 'I've been hoping that wasn't the reason you came back.'

'It's the only reason. To find out the truth.'

'The truth?' She smiled wistfully. 'You say the word as if it has magical properties, JonJo. There are more important things in life than the truth.'

'I don't understand.'

'It doesn't matter. Can't we forget it?' she said hopefully. 'Can't we just leave it in the past?'

'But that's the point, Abby. It hasn't stayed in the past.' John-Joseph got to his feet and paced the floor. 'It's travelled with me, lurking in the background somewhere, every day of my life.

'Even when weeks and months go by without me thinking of you, it's still there, somewhere down at the bottom of this great, deep well. And I know that eventually it's going to come to the surface again and for a brief, empty moment I'll ask myself why. Why did it happen?'

He stopped pacing and looked out at the broken blackness of the night. She watched him, misty-eyed, as a new ache took its place beside the others she endured.

'What difference can it make?' she said regretfully.

'If it makes no difference, why won't you tell me?'

'Because I don't want to.'

He turned from the window and stared at her. 'Then there is something to tell?'

'No! Nothing!' For a moment, in her exasperation, some of her old fire was there again. 'I told you everything!'

'Not everything!' John-Joseph retorted. 'Not anything!

'It wasn't your dad,' he said, more thoughtfully. 'I know he didn't like me but that wasn't it. That wouldn't have made you do it!'

'Did you really travel all this way just to have an argument with me?'

'I hope not!'

Without them realising it, their voices had become more strident.

'What made you do it, Abby?'

She pulled herself to her feet and walked away from him across the conservatory. It gave her time to steady her nerves, to put out the old fire and to compose herself.

'It was a long time ago. Forty years. I don't remember.'

Even across the room she could see in his eyes that he didn't believe her. 'You know,' he said. 'You were a much better liar back then.'

He said it half-jokingly. Given the chance it would have made her smile. But Eleanor was in the doorway with a glass of water and some pills for her mother.

She strode into the conservatory and went

to Abby's side. She glared at John-Joseph and spoke to him as the intruder she considered him to be.

'Mr Delaney, I think it's time you were leaving!'

As he went through the front door and down the steps, John-Joseph heard Abby's voice behind him.

'It was wonderful seeing you. Promise you'll come again. Promise!'

There was an urgency in her voice, a painful longing. Pleased, John-Joseph spun around to say of course he'd come again, then realised that the words had been meant for Michelle. Abby was hugging her daughter fiercely, as if her arms were trying to swallow the young girl whole.

Michelle murmured an inaudible reply and slipped away. Abby brushed at her eyes with the back of her hand.

John-Joseph watched her, foolishly disappointed. She loved her family, it was clear, with an intensity she had once reserved for him.

He stood at the foot of the steps trapped in a tangle of emotions, caught in two minds, unsure of what to say or how to leave things.

Abby read at a glance all that was written on his face, and came to him.

'You, too, JonJo,' she said. 'Come again – tomorrow. Please. I'd like you to.'

Unconvinced, he took her hands. 'Are you sure, Abby? Is that really what you want?'

'It is,' she said. 'More than you can possibly imagine.'

She spoke softly, too quietly for anyone else to hear. This moment was theirs alone. A few seconds of intimacy between them. John-Joseph felt ridiculously happy. Suddenly unable to trust his voice he nodded brusquely, then turned and walked smartly down the drive.

Eleanor was waiting beside the car. She clearly didn't echo her mother's sentiments.

'Well, you've seen her, Mr Delaney. It must be obvious to you that any unpleasantness, any shocks or exertions, aren't good for my mother.

'It would be better if you didn't come again.'

Still giddy with delight at Abby's words John-Joseph took a moment to compose himself.

'I'm sorry, Eleanor,' he said, a little more gruffly than he intended. 'I don't think it would.

'Besides, it isn't your decision. It's your mother's. And it's one she's already made.'

He thanked Eleanor for her hospitality, though it did nothing to thaw the frostiness of her expression. Then he jumped into the car beside Michelle.

Abby watched from the house, sorry to see him go. Sorrier still that she hadn't been able to tell him what he wanted to know. But she'd had no choice. Because she knew that the answers he was looking for still had the power to hurt him, even after all these years.

And she believed what she'd told him. There were more important things in life than the truth.

Like family.

Like faith in one's family.

Her father had changed.

'Don't lie to me, Abby!' he roared. 'I want the truth!'

Abby was shaken. She'd never seen her father so angry. Or so genuinely worried.

'How do you know Frank Delaney?' he demanded.

'I don't!' Abby was adamant. 'I've never met him!'

'You were seen in his car! That American thing!'

'I was with JonJo!'

'JonJo?' Her father scowled, confused. 'What's he got to do with it?'

'He's Frankie's brother,' said Abby. 'You'd know that if you ever talked to me about him. If you'd ever listened!'

'He's a Delaney? The boy's a Delaney? Are you mad, girl?'

'What does that matter?' Abby was genuinely bewildered. 'What difference does it make?'

Her father took hold of her shoulders, remarkably gently considering how upset he was.

'Listen to me, Abby. Frank Delaney is scum! He's a vicious criminal! He's got a hand in every rotten deal in the city! Protection, loan sharking, robbery with violence – he's into the lot!

'And that kind of thing runs in the family!'

This was too much for Abby. 'Not JonJo!' she protested. 'He's not like that!'

'They're ALL like that,' her father insisted. Was this the policeman in him talking? She didn't know. He'd never spoken to her like this before – she'd never heard him speak like this to anyone.

'Their father can't show his face anywhere in town! He's got so many people after him, on both sides of the law, he's afraid to set foot on dry land! The whole family's rotten to the core!'

Suddenly his anger was replaced by an icy

calm. A grim determination. 'Get rid of him, Abby! Get rid of that boy, or I'll make you!'

But Abby, too, was capable of quiet determination. She watched the disapproval harden her father's face, and she stood firm.

'I'm sorry, Dad,' she said. 'You're wrong. It'll take more than that to make me give up JonJo!'

She didn't know it then, but there was more. A lot more.

Enough to bring her whole world crashing down.

CHAPTER FOUR

Abby woke next morning with an unfamiliar sense of anticipation. JonJo was coming. They would go out somewhere. They would spend time together. They would talk about themselves and about their lives. They would recount, they would remember and re-live.

For a few minutes she felt like a nervous schoolgirl, looking forward to a first date.

But her body protested as she got out of bed, and the aches and pains reminded her she was no longer a naïve, impetuous young girl. Far from it. And JonJo wasn't the boy she'd fallen in love with 40 years ago; was no longer the gauche teenager she had given her first kisses to.

Indeed, he was no longer JonJo.

He was, instead, John-Joseph Delaney, a man she barely knew. A serious man, full of important questions she didn't want to answer.

But she knew that he deserved to have them answered. Even if the smile that melted her heart had faded in the lines of the years. Even if he didn't still have the power to make her stomach flip over and her legs go weak.

Even if he wasn't JonJo any more.

But then, if he wasn't that same JonJo, why did she dress and do her hair and put on her make-up with such unusual care and attention that morning?

At half past ten Eleanor came into the conservatory.

'Your date's arrived,' she said, with that unnerving capacity she had for reading her mother's thoughts. It had been easier than ever today.

'Mum,' she continued anxiously as she followed Abby through the house. 'Are you sure you should be doing this? Seeing him? Raking up the past?'

'I'm not sure at all,' confessed Abby. 'But not for the reasons you think.'

'Then why do it? Why distress yourself?'

Abby stopped in the hall and faced her daughter.

'Because that's what life is all about,' she said with certainty. 'Taking chances. And because I am still alive, Eleanor.'

She smiled, determinedly and brightly, to reassure her daughter AND herself.

Then she opened the front door, and that's when commonsense and clarity and all things sane and normal fled her world.

John-Joseph stood on the driveway beside

an enormous American car. A bright blue Cadillac convertible, polished and sparkling and almost as wide as his smile. He gestured towards it with a theatrical sweep of his arm.

Speechless, breathless, almost without thinking, Abby slipped inside when John-Joseph held open the door.

Eleanor hurried down the drive with her mother's coat and scarf.

'Don't worry!' John-Joseph said chirpily as he walked around the car. 'I'll have her home by twelve!'

'I'll make some lunch then,' Eleanor said, pleased.

'I wouldn't,' John-Joseph retorted. 'I meant midnight!'

John-Joseph chuckled, Abby laughed, and the Cadillac slid away leaving Eleanor watching anxiously from the drive.

Sinking into the soft leather upholstery, Abby shook her head in amazement.

'Where on earth – how on earth – did you get this?' She gasped.

'Contacts!' John-Joseph said enigmatically.

Then he smiled a smile that did a pretty good job of melting Abby's heart and making her legs go weak.

She had, he thought, grown paler overnight. The shadows round her eyes were more pronounced, try as she had to conceal them, try as she might to smile them away.

'You must tell me if it's too much,' he said. 'Tell me when you want to rest.'

'You're beginning to sound like Eleanor,' she scoffed.

Even so, he persisted. 'How bad is it, Abby?'

Perhaps it wasn't the kind of question he should have raised. But he needed to know. And when there was something he needed to know, he just asked. It had been his habit for years. 'Are they doing everything they can for you?'

'Everything,' Abby replied, 'and more. And it's still not enough. There's not enough rest in the world for me now, JonJo.'

Abby gazed out of the window at the passing streets and spoke wearily.

'Living with Eleanor is hardly like living at all,' she admitted. 'She won't let me do anything for myself. I can't go out alone. I can't shop alone. I can't sit by an open window without her closing it.

'You have no idea,' she said, 'how much I've longed for a breath of fresh air! And then you came along.'

She turned her head to smile at him, and John-Joseph felt his heart swell up. He found himself almost bursting with pleasure.

Everything he'd done – his journey half way round the world, his search for Abby – the whole preposterous idea – had been made worthwhile by her words.

He felt younger than he'd done in years.

'And of course,' Abby continued with feeling, 'she won't hear of me going to the football!'

'Football?' John-Joseph echoed the word in disbelief.

Abby grinned enthusiastically. 'Oh, yes!

It's something I really got into when I met my husband. I'm an Everton supporter. We're on the verge of having a really good team again!'

As quickly as her enthusiasm had risen, it waned again.

'But Eleanor's made it off-limits, now,' she said. 'I don't have the strength to fight her and the illness.

'Besides which,' she said, sighing sympathetically, 'she means so well and tries so hard. I don't have the heart to disappoint her. She'd do anything if there was anything she could do – but she can't. No-one can.'

'Are you absolutely sure?' John-Joseph asked. 'There are always new techniques, new drugs, here, or abroad. If it's the money, Abby, I have money, couldn't we – isn't there something–?'

He hadn't meant the day to start like this, but there was an urgency in his voice that he couldn't begin to conceal.

Abby interrupted him softly.

'We've tried everything, JonJo. We're still

trying. It's all this family has thought about for years.

'I haven't given up. I'll never do that. Especially,' she said, looking at him openly, 'not now!'

She squeezed his hand. 'But I don't want to talk about it. Not today.'

She turned in her seat to face him, and there wasn't a trace of self-pity or anger about her.

'Today is for life. And for living,' she said happily.

John-Joseph glanced over with a look of longing and apology. When he turned his eyes back to the road they had all but misted over. He swallowed hard and nodded briskly.

'Just like every day we ever shared,' he said.

Turning the wheel he pointed the automobile towards Port Sunlight.

As they relaxed into each other's company past and present merged.

They drove for 20 minutes, and travelled 40 years.

Hulme Hall, Port Sunlight Village. 1963. The last time The Beatles played there. The first time JonJo drove the Bold Street Boys in his brother's new car.

Colin couldn't believe his eyes when JonJo and Abby pulled up at his house in the ice-blue convertible.

Dillon immediately stubbed out his cigarette, scared of dropping it and spoiling the car's immaculate interior.

Bomber, wicked as ever, telephoned ahead to the hall. In a mock American accent he said he was a big US record producer, the biggest, keen to, 'mosey along and see this little English band!

'Could y'all keep us the very best seats in the house? And a place in the car park as well?

'On seconds thoughts, buddy,' he drawled, 'make that two places in the car park, if y'know what I mean!'

The Cadillac made a huge impression when it pulled up outside the hall. Until, that is, four Liverpool scallies climbed out of it, followed by Abby and Susan trying hard not to giggle.

The manager, who had taken Bomber's call, found it easier than the girls to keep a straight face.

'And which one of you is Elvis?' he enquired.

John-Joseph parked the car and they walked the quiet streets of the beautiful garden village. He took her hand this time without a second thought.

They had a lot of catching up to do. A lifetime's worth. Two lifetimes. His and hers.

'When you and I broke up I guess I lost the plot,' he said. 'I dropped out of art school. Got into a few silly scrapes. Nothing serious. Trivial stuff. But I couldn't get out of the rut I was in. So I took the plunge and joined the merchant navy.'

'Yes, I heard that,' Abby said, 'from Susan. She still saw Bomber once in a while. I couldn't believe it when I heard you'd gone.'

'Well, there was nothing to keep me here, was there?'

'What about your family?'

'What about them?' John-Joseph snorted. 'I never did see anything of Dad. When I finally left home, Gran went back to Ireland. She'd always wanted to. She had cousins and sisters still living there.'

'And Frankie? What happened to him?' Abby couldn't keep a tremor of anxiety out of her voice.

'I've no idea,' John-Joseph said, not noticing her apprehension. 'He moved to London and we quickly lost track of each other. He wasn't even at Gran's funeral.'

'So in the end,' she said gravely, 'you lost everyone. Not just me.'

'Not quite everyone,' John-Joseph said, and suddenly he laughed with genuine amusement and affection. 'I couldn't get rid of Colin. He joined the navy with me!'

'Colin did?'

'Said he couldn't let his best friend face the

world alone. We travelled thousands of miles together on a dozen different ships. The crazy fool couldn't even swim! He still can't!

'Eventually, when we'd had enough, he settled in America. I settled in Australia. We went into business together, importing classic American cars for the Pacific Market.

'Things really took off. We expanded throughout the southern hemisphere, and now...'

He stopped, suddenly aware of how pompous and impersonal he sounded. He smiled, sheepishly apologetic.

'You wouldn't believe how well we did,' he said, faintly embarrassed. 'Now I've got contacts all over the world, a very comfortable lifestyle, two homes...'

'But no family,' Abby said, gently persistent. 'You never married?'

John-Joseph shook his head, and shrugged again as if, with this, he could dismiss the disappointments of a lifetime.

But Abby wouldn't let them be dismissed.

'Is it my fault, JonJo? Am I to blame?'

'Of course not! How could you possibly be? Marriage just didn't happen for me, that's all. I came close a couple of times.' He laughed a little grudgingly.

Involuntarily, he conjured up a mental picture of two former fiancées, and one former secretary who, he knew, had loved him more than most.

He'd never let on that he knew about her feelings. He'd always been afraid that she might take it the wrong way. Hope would have been the unkindest thing to give her.

Abby saw how far his thoughts had taken him, and she deliberately chuckled to lighten the mood.

'Oh, I'm sure you've had your conquests,' she said. 'I know what you sailors are like. A girl in every port!'

'Not quite.' John-Joseph smiled raffishly. 'Although I once had a rather special one in Liverpool.'

JonJo took his special girl to The Cavern – every Wednesday night – where they saw the best group in the world and tried to dance in a space that seemed no bigger than the back of his brother's convertible.

Later, when the Bold Street Boys had drifted home, he and Abby often drove into the countryside. Lying side by side on the hood of the car they stared up at the sky, lost for what seemed like hours among a million stars.

Not one of them shone brighter than their love.

In the small hours of the morning he took Abby home, then left the car at Frankie's flat before cheerfully walking the four and a half miles to the modest terraced house where he lived with his gran.

The stars, and his thoughts of Abby, saw him home.

He took her to The Cavern again. John-Joseph paid the entrance fee to the Beatles' Exhibition and he and Abby descended the narrow steps together.

'I can't believe you've never been back

here,' he said. 'Why ever not?'

'I don't know.' Abby shrugged nervously. 'Too many memories perhaps.'

'Good memories, though.'

'Good, yes, of course. But bittersweet, JonJo.'

As they reached the foot of the stairs and stepped into the remarkable replica of The Cavern that had been built with so much care and attention, John-Joseph was suddenly aware of how much Abby's hands were trembling.

She had been completely unprepared for the rush of memory that threatened to overwhelm her. Everything she had ever remembered about the time and place came back to her. And everything she had ever forgotten.

The tiniest of details, closed to her mind for so long, burst open and flowered like buds in spring.

The way The Beatles used their amplifiers as tabletops, cluttering them with sandwiches, bottles and cigarettes. The way the edges were scarred with burn marks and the way the smoke hung like a false ceiling immediately beneath the bare bricks of the real one.

The way the glamour and style of the fans was always in stark contrast to the dinginess of the surroundings.

The way the air was filled with the smell of onions from the hot-dog stand and bleach from the toilets. The way the ventilation shaft and electric fans had never been enough to offset the stuffiness and keep the air clean. It could take days for the stench of The Cavern to leave your clothes and hair. And even longer for the memory of it to leave your mind.

Even longer than 40 years.

The emotional ambush of these sensations took Abby by surprise.

All at once she was back in 1963 hearing *She Loves You, From Me To You* and *I want To Hold Your Hand* for the very first time; remembering exactly what it felt like to be 17 in the best of times, and in the best of loves.

Tears stung her eyes. She'd been feeling

weak and light-headed all morning, with the excitement of the day she had thought, but now her legs threatened to go from beneath her altogether.

Concerned, John-Joseph helped her to a bench where she sat down heavily. She gripped his hand tightly.

'I'm sorry, I'm sorry,' she gasped.

'Don't be silly,' he reassured her, 'it'll pass.'

'No, I'm sorry,' she said, 'for everything! For hurting you, for breaking your heart. And I'm sorry,' she sobbed, in distress, 'for being selfish now!'

Suddenly she raised her head and the guilty, grief-stricken eyes of a 17-year-old gazed up at him.

'It's not fair of me, JonJo,' she said, 'but I want to tell you what happened all those years ago.

'I'm tired of being selfless and unselfish. I'm tired of letting Eleanor look after me because it's what she needs. I'm tired of being apart from Michelle because it's what she wants.

'I want to tell you, I have to tell you, because…' her voice was cracked, her sobs becoming harsher and more distressed … b-because I can't bear you thinking that I just stopped loving you!'

The summer of 1963. The most wonderful summer of her 17 years. In her young heart, Abby knew these were the best of times. She couldn't imagine a happier life. Unless, of course, it was one where her father accepted her love for JonJo and had given the couple his blessing.

For now she knew that wasn't going to happen. Her father's outspoken disapproval was the one, small cloud that darkened the unbroken blue of her perfect summer sky.

That's how she thought of it, her father's displeasure, as a fleeting storm, an inconvenient squall, that would quickly pass in a shower of rain, a flash of summer lightning, and a growl of thunder. Its passing would leave everything fresher and cleaner and better than before.

All she and JonJo had to do, she confidently believed, was hold to each other and wait for the squall to blow over.

At the end of June, JonJo's gran left for a holiday in Ireland, and so, for two weeks, the young couple found themselves with something they'd never had before. Something precious. A place where they could be alone together.

They made the most of it, spending almost every evening there. They didn't do anything special. Nothing out-of-the-ordinary. And yet, everything they did was special. Playing music, watching television lying on the floor with their heads together reading every gossip-column and magazine feature they could find about The Beatles.

Sometimes they sat apart in silence, Abby wading through her mounting homework, school books scattered across the kitchen table, JonJo sketching her from across the room, hardly taking his eyes from her, never quite capturing the mixture of concentration and contentment on her beautiful face.

Sometimes they talked into the long dark hours, making plans, making promises.

Once, she stayed the night.

Abby suspected that her mother knew the situation, but whether or not her father was aware of it she couldn't say.

A detective inspector with the CID, when Abby's father was in the middle of an investigation they could sometimes go for days with their paths not crossing.

This time Abby hadn't seen her father in almost a week.

Something big was on, but she didn't know what.

It was a Saturday night, stealing into the early hours of Sunday morning.

They'd been at the Tower Ballroom in New Brighton – she and JonJo and Susan and the Bold Street Boys. There, along with five thousand other Beatles fans, they had danced themselves to a standstill and screamed their throats raw.

Hours later, still dancing in her dreams, Abby lay in bed, half-wrapped in sleep, the memories of the day pulled round her snugly like a blanket.

Slowly she became aware of another person in the room. She opened her eyes and looked around.

Her father was in a chair by the window. She could see him faintly silhouetted by the streetlights through the curtains. He was sitting perfectly still, not moving a muscle. Only the sound of his breathing had alerted Abby to his presence.

'Daddy? Is that you? What's wrong?'

'Nothing's wrong, Abby. Everything's fine.' But the grimness of his tone contradicted his words.

'I'm sorry I haven't seen much of you lately,' he said. 'I've been busy. Last Wednesday around midnight, a man was seriously injured on the edge of town by a hit-and-run driver.'

Why was he telling her this?

'It was an accident?'

'No. It was deliberate. He was a petty, small-time crook, mixed up in a lot of bad business.

'It's taken time, but we have evidence now that the car was American. An ice-blue Cadillac. I'm ready to make an arrest.'

Trepidation clutched at Abby's heart as some of the pieces fell into place.

'Frankie?' she said.

Her father's words came through the darkness with an awful inevitability.

'No, Abby. I'm going to arrest JonJo!'

Nothing could have prepared her for the shock, the hammer blow that sat her bolt upright in bed.

'JonJo? That's ridiculous!' she cried. 'It wasn't JonJo! It can't have been!'

'I've got all the evidence I need,' her father said.

'You can't have!'

'I have a witness, Abby. An eye-witness who is prepared to swear in court that JonJo was driving.'

'But it can't be true.'

Abby's head was spinning. She felt as though she'd woken from a dream and straightaway plunged into an unfathomable nightmare.

'True or not,' her father said, 'my witness will say whatever I tell him to!'

And suddenly, in the chilling silence that followed, Abby understood completely what he was saying. This had nothing to do with police work, or the law. It was to do with her and JonJo, and splitting them up.

With trembling fingers the girl switched on her bedside lamp. She wanted to see the face of the man who was saying these terrible things. As if somehow it might be a stranger's face. It sounded, after all, like a stranger's voice.

But it was her father's face that gazed at her across the room, carved with the oddest expression of love and ill will.

Abby shook her head in desperation. 'I won't let you do it!' she threatened.

'You can't stop me,' her father replied.

'I can! I can say I was with JonJo! I can

give him an alibi for that night! For every night!'

'No Abby, you can't. Late Wednesday night, you were here. You were home with your mum and Aunt Dora. Remember? She stayed later than usual that night.'

'But from what I know of JonJo's circumstances, he was alone.'

Abby knew that her father was right. JonJo had been home alone. He'd told her so.

He'd had no early class on Thursday morning, so on Wednesday night he'd stayed up late and finished his sketch of her.

Alone.

'Like you, Abby,' her father said, 'I do my homework.'

Abby shuddered. The shock wore off and the tears began. Tears at the terrible unfairness of it all.

'You can't do this, Daddy! Don't! Please! I love JonJo!'

But her appeal fell on deaf ears, and her tears had no effect on her father's intentions.

'What do you know about love?' he said fiercely.

'You have no idea what it's like to love someone more than life itself. Wait till you have a child of your own, Abby. A daughter you've cherished and adored. A daughter who's about to throw her life away on someone who's just no good!

'Talk to me then about love. Tell me then what you feel. And tell me there isn't anything you wouldn't do to protect her. To save her from a family like that.'

He sat back in his chair almost calmly. There wasn't a shadow of doubt in his eyes.

'I'm doing this for you,' he said. 'I'll do whatever it takes. I'll ruin his life before I let him ruin yours!'

'I don't believe you!' Abby spluttered tearfully. 'I don't believe you could do that!'

Her father smiled coldly, smothering all the compassion he felt in case it should be mistaken for lack of resolve.

'Then you don't know anything about love,' he said. 'Finish things with JonJo. For good. Tell him it's over. Tell him you never want to see him again.

'Do it, Abby. Or I'll see him put away for a long time. And no-one will have the slightest doubt that he's guilty!'

The chair creaked as her father rose. He crossed quietly to the door.

'Daddy?' Abby's throat was tight with grief. 'I'll never forgive you for this.'

'Yes, you will,' he said gently, in a voice that was almost her father's voice again. 'Some day, you'll thank me for it.'

As sure of himself as he'd ever been, he slipped out of her room and closed the door. Abby remained sitting in bed, numbed by the awfulness of it all.

Alone in the pool of light from the bedside lamp, she began to shiver.

She knew it was the beginning of the end.

Summer was over before it had begun.

They left The Cavern in total silence. Abby's stunning explanation had rocked John-Joseph's world. Everything he thought he'd known; everything he'd ever believed, and believed in, had been shaken.

He didn't know what to say, and probably couldn't have spoken if he had known.

He drove out of the city aimlessly, and erratically for a while, before finally pulling over and confronting the terrible truth of it all.

It was too much information for him to handle all at once, too many shocks for him to take on board. His senses were reeling, he felt numbed and in shock, as if he'd been hit by a bus or been involved in a horrendous traffic accident.

His entire life had unravelled, and all he could do was pick feebly at a few loose threads.

'You're saying, Frankie tried to murder someone…?'

Abby nodded apologetically. Forty years ago, JonJo had worshipped his brother. Rather, he'd worshipped someone his brother had never been. 'But, attempted murder, Abby. How could your dad let

Frankie away with something so serious?'

'Dad said he was out-of-control. Becoming careless. Acting rashly. Making mistakes. He said it was only a matter of time before the police got him for something!'

'But, attempted murder, Abby! And your dad was going to pin it on me?'

John-Joseph was utterly incredulous.

Abby nodded dismally.

'I couldn't believe it myself,' she said. 'My father, my hero, who helped people and looked after them, was prepared to break the law just to stop us being together.

'Now I have girls of my own, I know the lengths I would go to protect them but that night all I felt was devastated – I'd lost you both.

'He'd have let your brother go free, knowing what he'd done, simply to force us apart.'

'And that's when you began avoiding me,' John-Joseph said. 'You stopped coming to The Cavern. You said you had to study for university. And at weekends, something always came up to stop you seeing me. A part-time job. Family obligations. There was always something.'

'I was just putting off the inevitable,' Abby said. 'I wasn't avoiding you, JonJo. I was avoiding that horrible moment when I'd have to finish things – until I couldn't avoid it any longer.

'Years later, I found out there was no witness – no clear evidence to point to Frankie, or you even, in this whole sad and sorry business...'

Suddenly she bowed her head and seemed to wilt before his eyes. She was frighteningly pale. The revelations of the day had taken their toll on her, both emotionally and physically, it seemed.

Alarmed, John-Joseph put his arm around her. She took his hand and squeezed it reassuringly.

'It's all right, I'm all right,' she said. 'We have to eat soon, that's all. I need somewhere warm, and quiet, to sit for a while.'

They found a welcoming little inn nearby,

with a real coal fire and only Sixties' music on the jukebox. Mostly The Beatles.

While a waitress brought them menus and served the drinks, an endless stream of Beatles' songs played quietly in the background.

They all seemed touchingly, poignantly, apposite.

There are places I'll remember All my life…

'For a long time I tried shutting them out of my life,' Abby said, when her colour and some of her energy had returned.

'It was impossible, of course. Do you know how hard it was to live anywhere in the Sixties, never mind Liverpool, without constantly hearing The Beatles?

'But it was just too sad. Their music held too many memories of what we'd lost, and what I'd done to you.

'But what choice did I have, JonJo? I couldn't contemplate you going to jail for who knew how many years? It would have destroyed you.

'I had to give you up! I had to! I didn't

know what else to do!'

She was genuinely agitated, the grief in her voice was real, and raw, and new, as if everything had happened just last week, last month, instead of 40 years ago.

JonJo reached across the table and grasped her hands.

He struggled to suppress the powerful emotions boiling in him. The anger and resentment. The feelings of bitterness and spite. The terrible sense of loss and waste and, almost worse than everything else, the sheer, overpowering, needlessness of it all.

Blinking back his tears of pity for them both he found his voice.

'Oh, Abby! Abby! You must have been so scared. And alone!

'But, don't you see – there was no need for any of it. You broke us up, you broke our hearts, for nothing!

'Your father wouldn't have got away with it. It was a ridiculous plan. Frankie would never have let me take the blame! Never!'

In the process of raising her drink to her

lips Abby's hand froze in mid-air. Then, clearly trembling, she put the glass down on the table.

'I'm sorry, JonJo,' she said. 'I'm so desperately, desperately, sorry!'

She could barely bring herself to look at him, her heart was aching for him, for all he still had to hear, all he still had to suffer.

'That's exactly what Frankie would have done. I know he would – he told me so himself.'

Frank Delaney lived in a modest apartment block that nearly commanded a breathtaking view of the Mersey, but didn't quite.

His flat had been tastefully decorated, neither too fussy not too cavalier. But the furniture he'd added was ugly and uncomfortable, the carpets inexpensive and old-fashioned.

There was little light and air about the place.

It seemed to Abby nothing more than a place for someone to sleep and to eat, then to leave. Someone filled, like the flat itself, with a dullness of spirit and little imagination.

It didn't seem to her at all like the heart of a criminal empire.

When she called on Frankie she found him with company. Two brutish, big-shouldered men with cruel eyes. When one of them openly leered at her Frankie rebuked him savagely. Then he took the young girl through to another room.

The kitchenette.

It was there she pleaded for him, for JonJo's sake.

It was there he chilled her blood, and dashed her hopes and openly laughed in her face.

'So the famous Detective Inspector Clark is just as crooked as the rest of us,' he snorted. 'Well fancy that!

'But what do you expect me to do about it?'

'If JonJo's arrested, you'll have to come forward,' Abby said seriously. 'If you were driving the car, or you know who was, you'll have to say so!'

'And why would I want to do that?' Frankie inquired.

'For JonJo. For your brother,' she pleaded. 'He could go to prison.'

'It would do him the world of good in my opinion!' Frankie sneered. 'The kid's too soft. He needs toughening up!

'It's hard out there in the real world, girl! The sooner JonJo learns that lesson, the better!'

He shrugged and shook his head slowly.

'Sorry, darlin'. I don't know nothin' about no hit-and-run. As far as I'm concerned, Jonjo had the car all night. Didn't bring it back until the morning. That's what I'd have to say if anyone asked me.

'You wouldn't want me to lie, would you?' He laughed again, horribly self-satisfied, then turned on his heel and showed a very frightened girl to the front door.

Forty years away, John-Joseph could hear the sound of his brother's laughter in his head.

Abby watched in fretful silence, full of sympathy, as he struggled to come to terms with this new bombshell.

She hated herself for the pain she'd caused him; for the weakness that had driven her to tell him everything; for every truth she'd spoken, every hurtful, loathsome secret she'd given away.

And still there was more to come. More than he could imagine.

But that was enough for now.

What she'd told him already had certainly destroyed his most-treasured memories, and had changed the very way he thought and felt about his past.

Yet what was still to come, she knew, had the power to alter the rest of his life, for ever.

CHAPTER FIVE

'I've no idea where my mother is,' Eleanor spoke into the phone. 'I've hardly seen her in the last three weeks!' She added, more than a little disgruntled.

His wife's tone of voice made Tony look up from his newspaper.

Eleanor's fingers were kneading the receiver as she held it to her ear. Agitated, she switched the phone from one hand to the other and back again.

'Of course I'll give her the message,' she said tersely. 'Just as soon as I can!'

She put the phone down firmly and took a deep breath to calm herself. Then she lifted the receiver again and began to punch out the numbers.

Catching Tony's eye, she said, 'That was the hospital.'

'Bad news about Abby?'

'When is it anything else?'

After listening for a moment, staring glumly into space, she put the phone down for the final time.

'She's forgotten to turn her mobile on again,' she moaned. 'Or she's left it off deliberately!'

Tony threw his newspaper aside and reached out to take his wife's hand. He pulled her gently on to the settee beside him. She slumped against him and he put his arm around her.

'I'm sure she's fine,' he said.

'I'm not,' Eleanor said, refusing to be reassured. 'How can I be, when I don't know where she is?'

'I believe,' Tony offered, a little reluctantly, 'they were going to a football match this evening.'

'Football?' Eleanor expelled the word. A deep scowl ravaged her brow and a twinge of anxiety tightened her mouth. 'Are you sure?'

Tony shrugged ambivalently, but he was sure. He was absolutely certain. It was he who had supplied the tickets, at his mother-in-law's request. But he wasn't about to tell Eleanor that.

For 18 months now Tony had watched his wife struggle to keep her mother from death, by keeping her from life. It had seemed to him quite the wrong way to go about things, but he would never have dreamed of saying so.

Within the last few weeks, however, the struggle had been taken out of Eleanor's hands entirely.

Since John-Joseph Delaney's arrival, Abby had spent less and less time sitting around at home, and almost no time at all with her daughter.

So, of course, Eleanor's rôle in life had changed. Now Tony watched her try to pass the empty hours, and to fill the void her mother had left behind.

He understood instinctively that this was a hole he couldn't fill. Not yet. One day, in the not too distant future, when the time came to help Eleanor move on, he would be able to. But not right now.

Right now all he could do was put his arms around his wife to comfort her.

'I'm the one who's looked after her all this time,' she grumbled, hating herself for doing it, hating herself for how selfish and petty she sounded.

'I'm the one who's spent weeks and months with her! I quit my job so I could be here for her!'

'I know, love. I know.'

'And now she spends all her precious time with him!

'It's not fair, Tony. It's cruel!'

'Perhaps not,' her husband said, full of sympathy and tact. 'Perhaps it's the opposite, Elly.

'Perhaps she's trying to help you let go…'

'Let go of it! Let go of it! Make the pass!' Everton's latest, greatest, teenage sensation had collected the ball on the halfway line, shrugged off one clumsy challenge, and set off on a bull-like charge towards the opposition goal.

In the stand, Abby lent her voice to the forty thousand other experts screaming advice or hurling abuse at the dashing figure in the dark blue shirt.

'Wide! Wide!' She screamed. 'Get rid of it! Pass the ball!'

The crunch could be heard a mile away as the wonder kid's progress was stopped in its tracks by the blatant body-check of a burly defender.

Abby leapt from her seat in a frenzy.

'Send him off, ref!' SEND HIM OFF!'

Having 'done her bit' she sat down with a look of satisfaction, and saw John-Joseph grinning at her.

'What?' she said breathlessly. 'Did you see that?'

'No, I didn't,' he admitted cheerfully. 'I was too busy watching you!

'You look wonderful,' he said.

'I feel wonderful,' she answered, slipping

her arm through his and laughing. 'I feel healthier, and happier, than I've done in – you cannot be serious, referee!

'He didn't even give a foul! Can you believe that?'

Instantly she was swept up in the game again. John-Joseph could only hold on to her arm and allow himself to be taken along for the ride.

Three weeks had passed since Abby had told him the truth about their past. The truth which, terrible though it was, had set him free.

However much she'd hurt him all those years ago, however badly she'd broken his heart, he knew now that she hadn't simply fallen out of love with him. The betrayals weren't hers. They had belonged to other people.

And they belonged to the past.

A past John-Joseph could finally leave behind. If he wanted to.

Over the last three weeks they'd done their share of visiting old haunts.

The concert halls and clubs and ballrooms, renewed and redeveloped now, or bulldozed and obliterated, where they'd followed The Beatles from week to week and from gig to gig.

The beaches and seaside towns along the coast, the old-fashioned promenades where now and again they'd spent the time and money of their youth.

On these promenades, as they'd done 40 years ago, they ate candy floss and popcorn, hot dogs smothered in onions and ketchup, and ice cream sundaes in glasses with long silver spoons.

Abby over-indulged shamelessly, smacking her lips and acclaiming the taste.

'It's wonderful! And wicked! I love it! Food that really *tastes* of something!'

John-Joseph was torn between watching her enjoy herself and wanting to take better care of her.

There was always somewhere else to visit, something else to see.

Like Penny Lane, with the shelter by the

roundabout where JonJo and Abby had first kissed, and where they dared to kiss again a lifetime later.

And there was always more catching up to do.

'I moved away from Liverpool as well,' Abby said, as they strolled along New Brighton's landscaped promenade, where the Tower Ballroom had been, where ferries crossed the Mersey and Liverpool Pier Head loomed across the water.

'I went to Oxford. Where I got a rather unexceptional degree.

'I still saw Mum. She visited, but I didn't speak to my dad again for years. I hated him for what he'd done to us.'

If she hated her father still, there was no trace of it in her voice.

'We were reconciled when my mother passed away. It brought me and Dad together,' she recalled. 'It helped us become close again.

'And so did my kids. He was a fabulous

grandad! He loved the girls. He absolutely doted on them.'

They sat together on a bench, John-Joseph changing sides and putting his arm around her to act as a shield against the blustery wind.

Abby didn't seem to feel the cold. She was wrapped in her memories.

'And he liked my husband, too. Which was ironic.

'I got married, you see, because I met a man who was remarkably like you. At least, I thought he was. He had your kindness, and your patience, and your impossible sense of fun.

'He was good to me, and we discovered a lot of things we both enjoyed.

'But he wasn't you, of course. And, when I finally admitted to myself that I liked him but didn't love him, well, I guess it must have showed. Because we slowly, quietly, undramatically, drifted apart. Then we divorced.'

Abby stopped talking. John-Joseph didn't

speak. They were both comfortable in the silence.

'It was all very amicable, and civilised, and terribly, terribly sad,' she said at last.

'The girls were devastated. That's really where my problems with Michelle started.'

She smiled scornfully and shook her head. 'You know, after what I went through with my dad I swore I'd never say a single word against her boyfriends! But I did! I couldn't help it! You should have seen what she brought home! One oddball after another!

'I had to bite my tongue so often I almost bit it off!'

She laughed affectionately, and then grew thoughtful and more serious again.

'Perhaps my dad was right about that. Perhaps there's nothing you wouldn't do to protect your kids.

'He never felt any remorse about what he'd done. Not once. Right up to the day he died he believed that he'd done the right thing!

'And eventually, I think, I forgave him. A little.' She sounded apologetic; almost ashamed. 'Which brought me a lot of pain because I felt I was betraying you all over again.'

'Of course you weren't! You never did!' John-Joseph squeezed her hand and grunted gruffly. 'What's done is done, Abby. It's behind us now. Let's leave it there.'

So they did. They got to their feet and walked to the promenade in search of a café and hot coffee.

And gradually, as the days went by, the present took priority over the past.

John-Joseph knew they could never get back the 40 years they'd lost. Would Abby even want them back? She'd had children, a family, a fuller life, emotionally, than he. She'd have more to lose if the power was theirs to turn the clock back now.

Besides, in the end, what mattered wasn't the last 40 years. What mattered was the time they had together now.

So they did things they'd never done before, and went to places they'd never been.

Like football matches; and the races at

Haydock Park. A trip to Belfast and a weekend in London, where they rode the Eye and saw a West End musical.

They ate in country inns and fancy restaurants, and sometimes at his hotel, where they talked into those long dark hours that once they'd filled with plans and promises.

On more than one occasion she stayed the night.

Living in the present proved something that living in the past could never have done.

It showed them how little they'd changed. It showed them that, all things considered, they hadn't really travelled very far.

Despite everything that had happened, despite the years and all the things denied them, they were still pretty much the same people.

She was still his Abby. He was still her JonJo.

And, as lovers sometimes do, they forgot how fragile happiness can be.

But they remembered late that night after

the football match.

Abby had tired more quickly than she usually did and didn't talk much about anything in the car on the way home.

Where Eleanor was waiting for them. 'The hospital's been phoning,' she said, 'about the operation.

'They have to do it soon. Or not at all.'

'I know,' Abby said, dropping heavily into a chair. 'The chemotherapy hasn't been working as well as they'd hoped.'

She looked a little pinched, and pale.

'All right,' she said, 'let's do it. The sooner the better.'

She glanced up and smiled at John-Joseph.

'One thing I've learned from these last three weeks. There's no time like the present.'

The room at the hospital was quiet, but not restful. Inside, time slowed until it crawled by imperceptibly. The world stopped; and the daylight, and the air, and life, and everything, was put on hold, and held its breath, and waited for time to pass.

Abby lay in bed and waited patiently. John-Joseph waited with her.

Outside, in the hospital corridors and the streets beyond, life and the world went on as usual, bustling, rushing to and fro, unaware of time and tide and waiting for no-one.

Tony had left to drop in at work and Eleanor had gone to make a phone call.

She reappeared looking angry and judgmental.

'Michelle still won't come! She says she can't! Now she won't talk to me and no-one's answering the phone!'

Eleanor had spent the morning and much of the previous evening berating her sister.

She looked at her watch and scowled. 'I'm going round there,' she said grimly.

'Don't fall out with her,' Abby begged.

'I'll bring her back if I have to drag her here!'

John-Joseph got to his feet while she was scrabbling in her handbag for her car keys.

'Why don't I go and talk to her?' he said.

'You stay here with your mum. Spend some time together. I'll see if I can't reason with Michelle.'

Abby nodded desperately. She looked gratefully at John-Joseph and then anxiously at her daughter.

Everyone in the room was well aware that reasoning with her sister wasn't Eleanor's strong suit.

'Yes, thank you,' she eventually conceded, 'that would be kind of you.'

Mildly embarrassed, John-Joseph smiled at Abby and slipped quietly out of the room. Then, slightly more embarrassed, he slipped back in.

'It might help if I knew where she lives,' he said.

It was a student flat in a modest terrace; ideal for two and seemingly filled with clutter enough for ten.

'You're wastin' your time! She doesn't wanna see you.'

'I understand that,' John-Joseph refused to let the young man rile him. 'But I don't believe she doesn't want to see her mum!'

Zack was about to slam the door in John-Joseph's face when Michelle said it was all right to let him in.

They faced each other across the attic-studio. Paintings and sketches were scattered on the floor. A guitar, and a tapedeck, and, oddly, a cello stood in one corner.

Zack made a point of turning his back and staring out the window.

Michelle stood by herself and John-Joseph saw her clearly for what she was. A little girl who was frightened of losing her mother.

'If you don't see your mum,' he said, 'especially today, then you'll regret it. And, believe me, I know about regret.

'If your mum and I had stayed together, we'd have taken each other for granted, and squabbled, and fallen out, and made up again, like millions of people do.

'But we didn't stay together. And I miss every squabble and cross word we never had – and so will you!'

The girl had no answer. She nodded but

couldn't meet John-Joseph's gaze.

'When your mum's gone – not today, not tomorrow, hopefully not for a good while yet – you'll regret every opportunity you didn't take to be with her.

'Especially this one!'

She spoke at last in a tearful rush, a breathless babble.

'I know that! Don't you think I know that? But I can't! It's just – impossible! I can't!'

Then she hurried from the room mumbling, 'I'm sorry! I'm really sorry!'

Zack turned from the window as the door banged shut.

'Now see what you've done,' he barked. 'Are you happy now?'

John-Joseph shook his head apologetically. 'Can't you talk to her? Make her see?'

Zack sneered. 'It's Michelle's choice! It's up to her! We don't tell each other what to do!'

But he spoke with the frightened resentment of someone who didn't actually know what to do.

'She needs help, Zack. Don't give her the excuse of choosing between you and her family.'

'They're the ones doin' that!' the boy said angrily.

'Then don't let them!' John-Joseph retorted. 'Fight for her!'

Whatever Zack had expected to hear it wasn't that. 'What?'

'Fight for her! Don't let anyone, or anything, come between you! Put up with anything, suffer anything, to be with her. If you love her!

'But if you don't; if it's just a casual fling, an ego trip, if it's just your bitterness towards her family that's keeping you together; then let it go. Let her go.

'Otherwise you've no idea how much pain you'll cause Michelle – perhaps even yourself.'

Zack showed him to the door and closed it quietly behind him.

It was, John-Joseph thought, an encouraging sign.

The waiting was almost over. A nurse looked in to say that Abby would be 'prepped' within the hour and taken to the theatre not long after.

As she left the room the young nurse passed Michelle in the open door.

This time there was no restraint, no adolescent masking of emotion, no hiding her true feelings. Wide-eyed and wordless, Michelle rushed to the bed and threw her arms around her mum, this time the only awkwardness was caused by the pillows piled up behind Abby and the blankets restricting her legs.

Abby clung to her daughter for minutes without speaking.

Eleanor, try as she might to sustain an expression of sisterly reproach, found herself moved to tears. She directed a trembling smile of gratitude towards John-Joseph. He smiled in return, pushed back his chair and left Abby with her girls.

Stepping out of the room he caught sight

of Zack at the far end of the corridor. Hunched in the folds of an outsized parka, the teenager was pacing back and forth behind the glass door to the stairwell.

On seeing John-Joseph approach he turned immediately and hurried down the stairs.

Fair enough, John-Joseph thought. One step at a time.

He clearly wasn't ready yet for socialising.

The waiting was over.

When the nurses came to fetch her, Abby kissed her daughters, encouraged them, and then looked urgently towards John-Joseph.

'I'm sorry,' she said. 'I meant to speak to you…'

'You were speaking to your daughters. And rightly so.'

'But there's something I have to tell you.'

'Tell me later.'

'But it's terribly important, and there may not be–'

'Later,' John-Joseph said quietly, but full

of confidence, without the slightest hint of any forced bravado.

Then he kissed her, told her he loved her, and let her go.

As they wheeled her towards the lift the young nurse held her hand and chatted freely.

'Sometimes,' she said, 'they have music in the theatre. Who's your favourite?'

'The Beatles of course,' Abby said, without a moment's hesitation.

'Oh, I don't know, if they go *that* far back...'

John-Joseph stood with the girls and they caught sight of Abby smiling as the door slid shut behind her.

The waiting began again.

For hour after hour the surgeons stretched themselves to the very limit.

For hour after hour Abby was their world.

And for hour after hour the people who were Abby's world, those she loved the best, waited together.

Hours that seemed to stretch interminably.

The sisters had coffee together. Eleanor took Michelle's hand across the table.

By the time they'd talked through everything – from the trivial things that had kept them apart, to the terrible thing that had brought them together – the waiting was over.

Back in the room where time stood still, Abby opened her eyes, just for a moment, and so sleepily that she couldn't see a thing. But she instinctively knew who was there, and she sensed they were smiling.

She smiled, too. Indiscernibly.

'I go all the way back to The Beatles,' she said, before drifting off again.

Eleanor and Michelle sat on either side of the bed, grateful to be holding their mother's hands.

But reality impinged on their relief. 'All we've done,' the surgeon said, 'is buy her a little more time. And not nearly as much as we'd hoped, I'm afraid.

'Six weeks. Perhaps ten.'

'Ten weeks?' Tony said solemnly.

'Perhaps.'

Together though they were, round Abby's bed, they all – John-Joseph, Tony, Eleanor and Michelle – reacted to the news as individuals, separate and apart from one another, hearing the surgeon's words in isolation; each of them, in that terrible moment, feeling wretchedly alone.

'There's no perhaps about it,' Abby said. 'I want to speak to JonJo *now!* Alone.' Her voice was weak but her will-power strong, strong enough to have cajoled – or bullied – the surgeon into letting her go home, no more than two days after her operation.

Under *strict* supervision, of course.

Well, under Eleanor's supervision, which meant the same thing.

'It'll have to wait!' Eleanor said. 'You mustn't have any stress or excitement. At least till you're back on your feet!'

'Well, if that's what it takes I'll get up

now!' said Abby stubbornly. She clearly wasn't in any condition to stand, but nonetheless she pushed the sheets away as if she was determined to get out of bed.

'Stay where you are!' John-Joseph barked. Michelle had just brought him to the room. 'Do what your daughter tells you!' he insisted.

'Which daughter?' Abby retorted wickedly.

Totally exasperated, but thriving on it, Eleanor left the room. Michelle winked impishly at her mother before following her sister out.

John-Joseph replaced the bedclothes and sat by the bed.

He was shocked. Abby looked worse than she had done before the operation. Worse, even, than she'd looked just yesterday; the day she'd been allowed to leave the hospital.

She was thinner. Paler. Almost white. As if all of the colour had been washed from her.

But the fire was back in her eyes. And so he smiled. She clearly wasn't going to spend what little time she had left in bed like this.

A few days more, she felt sure, and she would be up and about again.

'Eleanor has her child back,' she said solemnly. But then she softened.

'No, that's unkind. *I'm* the one who got my child back. Thanks to you. Michelle is living here for the time being, did you know?

'You gave my daughter back to me, JonJo.'

He took her hand. It seemed so thin, so very thin, wrapped in his own.

'So it's only right that, now,' she said, 'I tell you about yours!'

John-Joseph flinched, perplexed, as if he couldn't comprehend what she had said.

'We had a baby, JonJo,' she said quietly. 'Before I went to Oxford, I discovered I was going to have a baby.'

His heart leapt, and fell, and leapt again. His head spun. His mind raced like a runaway train.

'Mum was brilliant! She was there for me through it all. And we thought it would be for the best if I … gave her away.

'I gave our baby away for adoption, JonJo!'

It was a memory that would always have the power to make her cry. And she cried now. And John-Joseph felt the tears in his own eyes, too.

How much more could there be? He wondered. How much more of their past was waiting to torture them?

'I never got to hold her, JonJo! I barely got to see her!'

Abby stopped talking, to blow her nose and to try to stem the tears.

'But Mum was right, it was for the best! Our daughter's had a good life, JonJo. A happy life!'

'How can you possibly know that?' he asked.

'Because I finally weakened, and traced her,' Abby confessed.

'Mum had handled everything, you see. And when she died, I found that she'd kept records. Every document. And date. And notes of every conversation.

'So I found her. Her name is Rebecca.'

Rolling over, she took an envelope from

the drawer of the bedside table.

She gave it to John-Joseph. Inside was a sheet of paper with a woman's name, an address, and a phone number, written on it. No photograph, though.

'Did you ever try to see her?'

Abby shook her head decisively. 'I thought about it. But I realised, if she'd wanted that to happen, if she'd wanted to know about us, she'd have tried to find me!'

'I thought, perhaps, she wanted to let the past lie.

'I'd made one huge decision about her life. I didn't feel I had the right to make another.

'So I kept her name close to my heart. And the thought that, if I wanted to, I could call her any time, made things a little easier somehow.'

'Oh, Abby,' John-Joseph grieved, 'you've been through so much.'

'This,' she said, touching the envelope, 'this is the last thing I can give you, JonJo. What you do with it is up to you.'

'We'll talk about it when you're stronger,'

he said. 'Together we'll decide what we should do.'

She closed her eyes and nodded, and a few last tears spilled out.

'I've told you it all now,' she whispered. 'There's nothing more.'

She was desperately tired. Eleanor had been right. Abby needed to rest. John-Joseph kissed her sleeping eyes and slipped out of the room.

That night, sleeping in his hotel bed, John-Joseph went all the long way back to The Beatles himself.

The Beatles were playing The Cavern when the power failed.

This was a regular occurrence but no-one minded. Condensation from the walls and ceiling often found its way into the fuse box.

The short circuits were dramatic and explosive, and the darkness that resulted was pierced only by the glowing tips of a hundred cigarettes.

'Hang on! We'll go acoustic!' Lennon shouted from the stage, and while they fumbled to switch

guitars the light came on.

But something inexplicable had taken place.

Except for JonJo and Abby. The Cavern had emptied.

The crowd was gone, and when The Beatles played, the couple danced, a slow dance, holding each other in their arms.

Until the lights went out again.

This time the blackness was absolute and unbroken.

In the silence Abby kissed him and whispered, 'Goodbye.' And JonJo felt her dissolve right through his fingers.

When the lights came on The Beatles were gone. But so was Abby, leaving JonJo feeling dreadfully alone.

But this never happened, he told himself. This isn't a genuine memory. It's a dream!

It was a dream. And he awoke shivering in his hotel room with the taste of Abby's kiss still on his lips.

Without thinking he picked up the phone and dialled, and when Tony eventually answered, he didn't apologise for the late-ness of the hour.

'Tony,' he said abruptly. 'How's Abby? Is Abby all right?'

Half asleep, Tony coughed and cleared his throat. 'She's fine,' he said thickly. 'She's sleeping. We're all sleeping, John!'

'Check her, will you?'

'Do you know what time it is? It's nearly–'

'Check on her, Tony. For me.'

The phone was put down with a clatter, and then there was silence. A silence that lasted a very long time.

Much too long.

Before Tony came back to the phone, John-Joseph knew.

'John?' Tony's voice was trembling. He was deeply shocked and finding it hard to speak. 'John, it's Abby. She's – gone. Abby died in her sleep…'

'I know, Tony. I know. I was with her, you see.

'I was with her tonight. At the Cavern.'

At the funeral it was said that she'd gone

peacefully. With the look on her face of someone who had done all she'd wanted to do.

In the end there was no ten weeks. No six. She hadn't needed them. She'd said all there was to be said, and she had let go.

Eleanor would find it hard to do the same.

Tony would help her, of course, and so would Michelle.

Surprisingly, she turned out to be the stronger of the two. She spoke at the service. She spoke about her mum with love, and about their final days together with gratitude.

Zack didn't speak. To anyone. But he was there where Michelle needed him. With a hand on her elbow; and a nod of encouragement; and a suit that was made-to-measure – for somebody else.

When John-Joseph caught his eye, he recognised in Zack's expression something he'd felt, in himself, a thousand times. Every time he'd looked at Abby.

Every time she'd been waiting outside the

college and had run into his arms.

Every time he'd watched her dancing at The Cavern.

And more recently, when he'd seen her come alive at a football match.

It was the look of a once-and-for-ever love.

'I've lost her, Roddy! I found her, and lost her again!' He'd phoned his secretary in Australia and told her everything. And as she'd always done, in all the years she'd worked for him, in all the years she'd longed for him, Roddy knew exactly what to say.

'But you did find her. And she was happy, truly happy, that you did.'

'We both were,' he agreed.

'And so, what are you going to do now? About Rebecca?'

'I really don't know.'

'Oh, I think you do,' said the perceptive, ever-reliable, Miss Rodwell.

'But there's no guarantees she'll even want to see me!'

'And, of course,' she said incisively, 'that

stopped you flying half way round the world to look for Abby!'

John-Joseph had to agree she had a point.

'You're right, Roddy. You're always right.'

But it's easy to be right, she thought, when all you do is say what you know is in someone else's heart.

Much easier to be wrong, and hurt, when you say what's in your own.

'When are you coming home?'

'I'm not sure where that is any more.'

Miss Rodwell wasn't sure either.

But *she* knew that his life here, with her or with anyone, could never compare to his past life there, with Abby.

She was reluctant to put the phone down. There was a huge part of her that felt she might never hear from him again.

There was a silence, which she broke, eventually.

'You know I'm always here if you need me.'

'I know that, Roddy,' he said. 'I've always known that. And, I'm sorry.'

She put the phone down after all. No

point in holding on to it when she could no longer trust herself to speak.

'I'm sorry, too, Mr Delaney,' she sobbed. 'Sorry *we* were never seventeen together.'

They'd written to each other a handful of times. And spoke on the telephone once. Only then did she feel ready, or able, to meet him.

But not on her own territory. She didn't want him 'too close to home' just yet.

So they arranged to meet in the welcoming little inn where he and Abby had once eaten. The one with the real coal fire and only Sixties music on the jukebox.

Mostly The Beatles.

John-Joseph got there over an hour early.

His daughter, a little late.

Neither of them could remember ever being so nervous before. In all their lives.

John-Joseph's first sight of his daughter, as she stopped in the doorway and looked around to see if she could pick him out, was a crushing disappointment!

She didn't look a bit like Abby!

He'd expected, and hoped for, another Michelle. Someone who was the image of her mother.

But Rebecca Lowe had little of Abby about her. Not unattractive, not plain, but not pretty; she was sandy-haired and solidly built.

Her voice was husky, and it wavered nervously when she first spoke.

'Hello.'

John-Joseph felt deeply ashamed of his disappointment.

'Thank you for coming,' he said. 'It's wonderful to see you!' and it was.

They sat near the fire and a talkative waitress immediately fell upon them.

'What can I get you?'

'A whisky. Neat.' John-Joseph said.

'And for your daughter?' the waitress asked, as she turned towards Rebecca.

John-Joseph was utterly taken aback. 'How do you know she's my daughter?'

'You kiddin'?' the waitress said, 'she's your

absolute double!'

Of course she was. *Of course she was!!* How could he not have recognised *his* face. Softer, of course, and much more delicate and feminine! And looking at him now with Abby's eyes, filled with Abby's gentleness and warmth.

'It's – it's wonderful to see you,' he said again. 'Properly!'

She laughed heartily. The ice was broken and immediately melted away.

'I brought some pictures of me and Harry and the kids,' Rebecca suddenly remembered, going into her bag for a couple of photographs.

'I thought you might like to have them.'

'I certainly would.' John-Joseph gulped, taking the pictures from her in trembling hands.

'What – what should I call you then?' she asked uncertainly. 'Not Dad–?'

'Not yet!' John-Joseph agreed. 'I haven't earned that right yet!'

He pondered for a moment, and then

smiled. 'Call me JonJo,' he said. 'That's who I am. It's who I've always been.'

'And, my mum?' Rebecca said, with hope, and real affection. 'Who was she? What was she like?'

Unprepared for the rush of emotions that hit him, John-Joseph could hardly begin to speak. He got clumsily to his feet in need of a moment to gather his thoughts.

Resting his hands on the jukebox to steady himself, he suddenly grew calm, and straightened, and smiled in a way that was both joyful and melancholy.

He spent his pound. And pressed the buttons.

Well she was just seventeen, you know what I mean,

And the way she looked was way beyond compare.

John-Joseph returned to the table and sat with his daughter.

A little while ago he'd travelled half way round the world to find his past. Now he had found his future.

This Large Print Book, for people
who cannot read normal print,
is published under the auspices of
THE ULVERSCROFT FOUNDATION